Saint He
I Hope y
my Book
J[illegible]

THE AMAZON DRIVER

JAMES ELLMAN

ISBN: 9798853172258

DEDICATION

I dedicate this book to the more than a million Muslim people who have been detained in reeducation camps since 2017. Most of the people who have been detained are Uyghur, a predominantly Turkic-speaking ethnic group primarily in China's northwestern region of Xinjiang. Experts estimate that reeducation efforts began in 2014 and were drastically expanded in 2017 and still exist today. There are verified reports of ongoing widespread discrimination against Uyghurs and other persons belonging to mostly Muslim minorities. Severe restrictions have been established by the Chinese government on Uyghur culture and the exercise of basic human rights and fundamental freedoms that include the right to freedom of religion or belief. There are copious confirmed reports of torture, cruel degrading punishment, forced sterilization, sexual and gender-based violence, forced labor, and forced separation of children from their parents by authorities. This is all being done under the guise of reeducation and training. But it is nothing more than government approved internment and concentration camps.

After World War II and the tragedy of the Holocaust, the world adopted a phrase that expressed its newfound resolve: "Never again." Never again would the world stand by and watch an entire people or group be targeted for extinction. Never again would the world allow genocide without consequences. In response to this resolve, The United Nations Convention on the Prevention and Punishment of the Crime of Genocide was signed in December 1948. Article II of the convention provides five examples of genocide with the intent to destroy, in whole or in part, a national, ethnic, racial, or religious group. All five of these examples have been met. Yet today the Uyghur people are experiencing these horrors and atrocities.

CONTENTS

ACKNOWLEDGMENTS

Thank you to my wife Ola for the tremendous effort, dedication and the many hours she spent in the editing of this story. This project would not have been possible without her involvement. She has always been supportive in my artistic endeavors like the piece of my artwork I used in the design of the book cover.

PREFACE

Each day Amazon Drivers deliver packages with unknown contents to over 100 countries and they never really know what is inside any of the packages they are delivering. Occasionally, something strange occurs during the delivery process. Perhaps a package makes a noise or even moves. In this story while making deliveries near Los Angeles International Airport an Amazon driver hears a noise in the back of his Amazon van. What he finds changes his life forever and others are very interested in the package. Because the Amazon driver has certain information, skills, and confidence he becomes a target of interest with the FBI and the mob. But his primary interest is protecting the package. As he does the story unfolds and elicits suspense, excitement, surprise, anxiety, and even a little romance and humor.

CHAPTER ONE

THE PACKAGE

Mr. Richards, first of all may I call you Walt? Yes, of course. Let's start with why you want this job. Mrs. Kaster my reason for applying for a job with the Bureau is complex. It would be very difficult for me to give you a short answer. I don't know if you want to hear my entire reasoning or if you want a quick answer. But if you want the quick answer it is because I want a job that is security work related, has job security and provides me with personal security. Walt, this is the strangest response I think I have ever received in conducting a job interview while employed here in Human Resources for the Bureau. I need to know what you mean by you want a job that provides you with security protection. I understand Mrs. Kaster but it requires a very long explanation and I don't know if you have the time. Long or short I think you need to be very specific in explaining your employment history and what you mean by your statement that you want a job that provides you with personal security. We here at the Bureau are not in the business of providing employees with security protection. However, I want to hear your entire explanation because as you know the Director explicitly requested that I interview you. For this reason alone obviously, I need to be especially thorough since the Director is involved. So yes Walt, I want to hear the entire story and your reasoning. Take as much time as needed because in addition to this employment interview I understand that there may be a related FBI investigation underway and what you tell me may be pertinent to that investigation. I have been asked by our investigation team that if there is something that you reveal during our interview pertinent to that investigation then I should ask you related questions. Also, I will be taking notes and what I learn I will report to the investigation team. If my interview with you takes several meetings it will not be a problem.

So Walt, let's take a different approach to starting this employment interview. Please tell me why you want to leave your current employment with Amazon since you have only been working there for six months. I want you to be specific and explain what kind of security work you performed for Amazon. Mrs. Kaster my job with Amazon had nothing to do with security work. My job title is Delivery Associate or better known as an Amazon Driver. Let me interrupt you Walt and state that the job you are applying for with the Bureau specifically necessitates in the minimum requirements that you have a bachelor's degree and at least two years experience in security related work. In reviewing your application for employment I see that you have the bachelor's degree but being an Amazon driver is not security related work. I am having difficulty continuing with this interview because you do not meet the minimum requirements. Yes, I know but my prior work experience with my other two employers before working at Amazon was clearly two years security related work. Additionally, while working at Amazon I was involved in a controversial shooting that got national news media attention a couple of months ago. In fact, the incident was reported on major television networks and newspapers across the United States. It was considered a very unusual shooting and it became a "Human Interest Story" that got lots of hits on the internet. Multiple public agencies were involved in the investigation including the FBI. The Bureau became highly interested in me. This is how I met Agents Brett Michaels and Chad Daniels. Both Agent Michaels and Daniels interviewed me while I was in jail. I provided them with information that was helpful to them. They had very recently begun a surveillance of Ricardo Sanchez because they suspected he was involved in sex trafficking in Las Vegas.

After I got out of jail I secured copies of incriminating documents which would significantly augment the FBI investigation of Ricardo Sanchez. I telephoned Agent Daniels and explained to him that if I could provide him with incriminating documents could he get me a job interview with the FBI. He did not know that I already had the documents in my possession. He said that he would do his best to get me the job interview if I provided him with the documents. I then gave him the documents the same day. Somehow the documents got the attention of your Director and now I am very pleased to be participating in this employment interview with you. Would you like me to tell you why Agent Michaels thought I might be a good candidate for the FBI? No, not yet, just go on with your story and be complete.

I want you to know Mrs. Kaster what I am about to tell you is everything that transpired and you will be the first one and only one to know the truth of everything that happened since I began work as an Amazon driver. No one knows the entire story-not Mr. Michaels, Mr. Daniels or even my parents. I am telling you because I really need this job with you and it would be irresponsible of me not to tell you the truth. As I said before my job title with Amazon was Delivery Associate or better known as an Amazon Driver. I worked four days a week, ten hours per day. Generally, I start work at about 9:45 in the morning and I finish work at 8:15 in the evening. I get a half hour for lunch and two fifteen minute breaks. I don't always take my breaks other than going to a restaurant or gas station to use their bathroom. When the weather is nice I sometimes eat my lunch in my Amazon van. If I am lucky I get a Prime van but fifty percent of the time I get a plain white van. There are pros and cons of getting a Prime van.

The pro is it is more comfortable and easier to move around inside the back of the van. Also, when delivering at night people are less likely to be concerned with a Prime van than a plain white van driving in their neighborhoods. Some drivers say that the disadvantage of driving a white van is that customers can more easily identify the driver by looking at the Amazon van license plate. This supposedly helps them when they want to make a complaint. But there are very few complaints and I have never had a complaint in my two months working for Amazon. So, it makes very little difference to me what kind of van I get assigned to me because I really like working for Amazon. They treat me very well. Plus the people I work with are all likable and I have made a couple of friends. These are not good friends but rather someone to have an occasional beer with after work.

All drivers are assigned a scanner. It's called the rabbit. The rabbit monitors drivers and enables Amazon to update customers on an order's location or delivery through a tracking service. It also gives step by step directions enabling drivers to do their work effectively.

Each driver is given a route and my route was in the Westchester and Inglewood area of California. Both cities border Los Angeles International Airport or better known as LAX. Also drivers are expected to load totes into their assigned van. The totes are actually boxes and sometimes called bags. The colors vary but I want you to know that they are big enough for a small size person to sit in with the lid closed. They are more like a large soft sided square picnic cooler box with a flip top. Each bag or box contains packages of various sizes. Normally vans are empty prior to loading, but not always. Most of the time packages are light weight but some can weigh as much as thirty pounds. So loading the boxes into the van can be tiring. Larger packages are delivered by an Amazon specialty delivery service.

This is all very interesting Walt but I have no idea how your being an Amazon driver got news media attention a couple of months ago or why Deputy Michaels and Daniels interviewed you. I understand Mrs. Kaster but the reason I am telling you all of this is because of an unusual red tote box that was in my Prime van. I specifically remember the date because it was on Halloween 2017. While doing my deliveries I saw grade school children in the play yard at a school dressed up in their Halloween costumes.

Also, you need to know that I had only been working for Amazon a few weeks so I was not totally familiar with all the procedures. I knew that occasionally a driver can be assigned a rescue route. This is a route where a driver helps another driver with deliveries. So when I found this red box already loaded in the back of my van I thought I might be helping another driver or that it was some kind of specialty delivery. Anyway, I didn't think much of it and I loaded my boxes and then began my route at around ten that morning.

Shortly after leaving the shipping facility, I heard a noise in the back of my van. It sounded like a slight cough. I thought maybe someone had illegally packaged a pet like a dog or a cat or a small animal. I did not think much of it other than I would check it out after my Hilton Hotel delivery. I was a little behind schedule.

I normally do several deliveries at the hotels near LAX. When I got out of my van with my packages I forgot about the noise that came from the back of my van. I went inside the Hilton and did my delivery. When I returned and got into the front seat of the van I remembered the coughing sound and decided to check it out. So, I turned and got out of my seat and went in to the back of the van and stood there quietly and motionless for a couple of minutes and listened. I didn't hear any noises other than the loud overhead jets at LAX. I started to return to the front of the van and I remembered the Amazon red tote box that was preloaded in my van. I moved up to it and gave it a slight soft kick into the side of the box. I heard nothing at all. But I did sense there was something inside it between the box wall and the content area. I gave it another slight kick but this time a little harder thinking if an animal was inside it would make some kind of noise or move. But I did not hear any noise so I decided to move the box without opening the lid. As I began to slide it I could tell that it was heavier than any other box I had handled at Amazon and so I stepped away suspicious of what might be inside. I stood there again for a minute or so and still no noise. I decided to open the flip top of the box but I was worried if it was a large snake like a boa constrictor or maybe some kind of biting animal. I heard a couple of strange stories from fellow workers about animals in their vans and so I thought I needed to be very careful lifting the lid. I don't know if these stories were true or just drivers having fun with a new Amazon driver. Anyway, I picked up from the floor a long tube package that was about two feet long and was very light. I guessed that it had large photos rolled up in it or construction drawings. I used it to very carefully to slowly open the lid.

I jumped back because to my surprise I found an extremely frightened somewhat Chinese looking girl. I say somewhat Chinese because her big wide opened eyes looked more Middle Eastern or Turkish than Chinese. I guessed that she was about thirteen years old but later I learned that she was much older. I asked her what are you doing in my van and how long have you been here? She looked very scared as she stared at me and said quite clearly in English I don't know while still sitting in the box. Then she started to stand up and I could see she was wearing what looked to be a red baggy jogging outfit from the 1990's. She said nothing as she began to stand up. I asked her again what are you doing in my van? She was obviously very frightened and I sensed something terrible must have happened to her. She repeated I don't know as she stood up and then bent over and rubbed her knees. I was sure she must have been in some pain or discomfort after being cramped in that Amazon tote box. I had mind flashes of her illegally entering the United States on a small boat but then thought maybe she was a runaway or perhaps she was hiding from the law. I asked for a third time what are you doing here? Her eyes began to tear. She again said I don't know in English and then something in Chinese as she began to fully stand up. I said do you speak English? She said a little. Then she said something in Chinese followed by in English please please please. Then she stood up still in the box. My cell phone rang and she waved her hands excitedly and again she said please please please as if she did not want me to answer my cell phone but I did. It was my supervisor asking me when I would be making my delivery to the Marriott Hotel. He said that the rabbit reflected that I hadn't delivered there yet and the customer was anxious for the package. He asked if I needed any help. As I looked at her rubbing her knees I assured him that all was okay and that I was leaving momentarily for my delivery to the Marriot Hotel. I didn't say anything about the girl. I then motioned with my hands for her to sit down. I told her that I had to think about what I was going to do with her but I am sure she did not understand me and then she began to sit back down in the box. I motioned with my head moving it from left to right indicating for her not to sit in the box. Then I pointed to the moving blankets behind the front seat and motioned with my hand for her to sit on the blankets. Tears began to well in her eyes but she did not cry and she sat down on the blankets. I got in the front seat and drove off to the Marriott to make my delivery. As I was driving I realized that she was probably hungry so I said to her take this and I tossed behind my seat my bag of snacks which had two apples and a small bag of potato chips. She didn't say anything and I could not see her in my rear view mirror but I heard her open the bag and bite into one of the apples.

I completed my delivery at the Marriott Hotel and hoped that on my return to the van that she would be gone. But she stayed and ate both apples and all of the chips so I knew that she must have been very hungry. I still did not know what to do with her so I motioned with my hand over my lips for her to be quiet. She clearly understood and said nothing. I wondered if she needed to go to the bathroom and also how much English she could speak. I certainly did not want her peeing in my van. I couldn't communicate with her and I didn't know if she had peed in my van. I did several more hotel deliveries near the airport and then it was time for lunch.

I pulled up to a shady parking spot at McDonald's near the airport. I assumed that she spoke Mandarin because I recently learned on the TV show Jeopardy that it is the most common language spoken in China. I got out of my seat and kneeled down next to her on the blankets and she moved back and away from me. I then typed on my cell phone using Google Translate in Mandarin do you want to use the bathroom and are you hungry? She then moved closer to me and looked at my phone. I handed her my cell phone and she wrote back. Yes, please help me. I then typed we will go inside the fast-food restaurant and you should use the bathroom while I get some food for us to eat in the van. She understood but looked afraid and very hesitant. I wrote don't talk to anyone and if needed pretend you are deaf and dumb. I said if you get scared and don't know what to do look for me and I will handle it. She clearly understood and stared at me as if she were my subordinate or servant. I then told her not to worry that I will make sure no one bothers her and that she is safe with me. She gave me a very slight smile, nodded her head up and down and I could tell that she felt relieved because I was going to help her. Her eyes started to tear. But I could tell she was no longer frightened. She had tears of appreciation in her eyes.

We got into the front seats of the van and then move to the back of the van and sat on the blankets. I was very concerned that someone might see me with her in my Amazon van which would violate Amazon policy. I gave her a hamburger and French fries and she ate it all. While we were eating I typed into my phone when I asked you what are you doing in my van you said in English I don't know. How come you don't know why you are in my van? She wrote back that her English is very poor and when she does not know how to answer a question that is asked in English she responds with I don't know. She said she does this especially when people are talking fast in English because it is difficult to understand them. I then knew that she did speak a little English but probably not enough for me to understand her and why she was in my van. I then typed into my phone when I am done with work we need to decide what to do with you. She wrote back please hide me for one night so I can get some sleep and then I will leave you alone. I did not immediately respond but rather got back into the front seat and went on to do some more deliveries. About an hour later I again kneeled down next to her in the van as she sat on the blankets. She looked very tired. I typed on my phone I will hide you for one night but you will have to stay in the back of the van while I finish my job. Her eyes looked appreciative and she wrote back thank you and at the same time said in English thank you. Then I wrote you cannot come back to my work with me when I return the van. I told her that I have a small apartment that is not far from my work and that I will give her a key to go inside and hide. She wrote back thank you and she had a big smile on her face. I wrote please do not steal anything from me. She looked at me straight in the eyes and wrote I would never do anything like that. I wrote you can use the bathroom and shower if you want while I am gone and I will be back to my apartment at about 8:30 this evening.

I did the remainder of my deliveries and she sat patiently and quietly in the back of the van. At about 7:30 that evening it was almost dark and I felt it would be safe for her to be dropped off in front of my apartment building. I parked directly in front of my apartment and pointed to the front door, gave her my key, and then motioned with my hand for her to go inside. She said syey-syeh and I watched her go inside my apartment. I didn't know what syey-syeh meant but I assumed it meant thank you and later I found out that is exactly what it means only it is spelled xie xie.

I returned the van to the Amazon warehouse and then bought my favorite pizza with pepperonis and anchovies and a salad to go. When I got home I attempted to open the front door but it was locked and I didn't have another key. I knocked on the door and no answer. I knocked again and still no answer. I hoped I did not have to knock again because I did not want to bring any attention to other tenants in my eight unit apartment building. Then I could see that she was looking out the corner of the mini blinds and she recognized me. She opened the front door and her long black hair was very wet and so were the shoulders of her red baggy outfit which I later learned was a uniform. There was only one towel in the bathroom which was obviously not enough for her shower and to dry her very long thick black hair. Rather than looking through my cabinets for an additional towel she waited for me to return. This impressed me and I knew she could be trusted and that she would not steal from me. I motioned for her to come to my cabinet in the small hallway adjacent to the bathroom. I gave her another towel for her to dry her hair. She smiled and said syey-syeh but we did not talk, not because we didn't want to but rather because of the language barrier.

After she dried her hair I pointed toward my kitchen table and made a motion for her to sit down and eat. I opened the pizza box. I didn't know if she had ever eaten pizza. I took a bite out of a slice and handed her a piece and she tasted it but I don't think she liked it probably because of the anchovies. But I could tell she very much enjoyed the salad and appreciated me bringing her food. She said syey-syeh and then said in English thank you.

After we ate I motioned for her to sit at my computer with me. She sat down next to me and I typed using Google Translate is there anything you need? She typed back yes, toothpaste. I said I would give her a toothbrush and some toothpaste. I could tell she was very happy about being able to brush her teeth. I then asked what is your name and how old are you? She typed my name is Amatullah Abdulla and I will be twenty years old next month. I was very surprised because she looked much younger to me. I thought she was about fifteen but never almost twenty years old. I tried to repeat saying her name but each time I mispronounced it and she would nicely try to correct me. After a few tries she said Abdulla. I then said Abdulla and she moved her head up and down indicating yes. It is from this point that I started calling her Abdulla.

She then asked me what is your name and how old are you? I said my name is Walter Richards but she should call me Walt and that I am twenty-four years old. Unlike me she clearly restated my name Walter Richards. I then asked her if she wanted me to wash her clothes and that I could give her a long shirt to wear or a blanket until her clothes dried. She hesitated and then nodded with her head up and down indicating yes. I gave her a long t-shirt and aimed my hand at the bathroom for her to change. When she returned she looked even younger wearing my long Lakers T-shirt which hung to her knees. I put her clothes in my washer-dryer and then we went back to the computer.

I wanted to know why she was hiding in my Amazon van and where she came from but I could tell that she was very tired. In fact, she looked exhausted. So, I took her into my bedroom and made sleepy hands and pointed my finger at the bed. She shook her head indicating no and abruptly turned and went into the bathroom and locked the door. I realized what I did was stupid and I should have known that she might misinterpret my offering her my bed for her to sleep. I waited for a few minutes for her to come out of the bathroom but she didn't. So I got some blankets and a pillow and I put it by the bathroom door. I then knocked on the door and returned to my bedroom. I heard the door open, then close and then I could hear the door lock again. She slept in the bathroom all night.

Okay Walt, this is heartbreaking and interesting but we are getting close to lunch and I also have a meeting to go to. I want you to tell me how this all got news media attention and why Abdulla was not the one in the news. Also should we not finish today you need to know that I always pick up my daughter after school from her high school tennis team practice. I cannot be late and so we must finish by five. So can you speed it up a bit? Yes, I can and thank you for your time.

Mrs. Kaster before I continue don't you want to know why Agent Michaels thought I might be a good candidate for the FBI? Yes, please explain. Agent Michaels said that he was very impressed with how much information I secured during my one evening surveillance of Ricardo prior to the shooting. I learned during my short surveillance that Ricardo was most likely involved in illegal prostitution and probably sex trafficking of young women who were illegally here in the United States. Although, prostitution is legal in Nevada there are very strict certification requirements. Prostitutes must not only be at least 18 years old but they must be employed at their own free will. I believed that these women were being exploited and coerced by using their illegal status to be strippers and prostitutes. Agent Michaels and Daniels agreed with me. Also, both agents studied the investigation relating to my booking that was done by the Las Vegas police department. They told me that they were impressed with how I restrained Ricardo and his two associates in front of my parents' home. Don't you mean Walt how you beat the hell out of Ricardo and shot the other two? Yes, but you have to remember that they all had guns aimed at me. I was able to shoot Ricardo's two associates with his gun an without them firing one shot. That is true Walt.

I also understand that you illegally rifled Ricardo's office the day after you got out of jail. Yes, that is true too Mrs. Kaster. I found in Ricardo's desk drawer a list of young women who entered the United States illegally. This list got the attention of the Director because of its significant and incriminating value. It is believed that the list may enhance the FBI's current investigation of the Rizzo Family.

Walt, it is lunch time now and I have another meeting so would it be possible for you to come back let's say at one-thirty? Does that work for you? Yes, whatever time is needed I am available. Good and let's plan to discuss Abdulla's escape from China, the shooting and the media's involvement.

CHAPTER TWO

THE ESCAPE

It is one-thirty Walt and you are right on time. Please continue where you left off before lunch. Okay, the next morning I went into the kitchen to make some coffee. She was quietly sitting at the table. I pointed at the clothes dryer and she got her under-clothes and red baggy uniform and then went into the bathroom. She came back and said in English thank you. I said in English we need to get you some clothes but she didn't understand. She had no idea what I was talking about. I thought if she were to walk on the street or go to the store in her red baggy uniform she would look very out of place.

We ate some cereal and after I motioned for her to come over to the computer. Using the computer I asked her if she slept okay. I tried to explain to her that I wanted her to sleep on the bed and that I was going to sleep on the couch. I said I think you misunderstood me and I only wanted you to get a good night's sleep. She wrote back that she didn't know what I wanted of her and that she slept well in the bathroom. I then asked her why she was in my van. She wrote back a very long explanation which took her almost fifteen minutes. While she was typing I cleaned up the dishes and shaved.

When I returned I could hardly believe what she wrote. She said that she is from Xinjiang, China. She is Uyghur which is an ethnic minority that primarily lives in the northern part of China. She said that the Chinese government would very much like to eliminate all Uyghur people. She explained to me that on July 15, 2017 she and her younger sister were separated from their family and placed in a Vocational Education and Training Center. However, the Center was nothing more than a labor internment camp where they attempt to reprogram Uygur's to erase their customs, heritage and religion. She said that Uyghur villagers of all ages fear being detained in Xinxiang. She said that parents especially fear their children being detained because it is sometimes more common than adult detention. However, the fear was always there for everyone in her village.

Prior to being detained and leaving her village she was working and studying to be a school teacher with a specialty in early computer learning for children. Her mother and father were agricultural farmers in Xinjiang raising wheat and melon crops. She said that her younger sister Patime died in the detention camp about a month after arrival with a mysterious ailment. She was only fifteen years old. She thinks her sister was poisoned because she complained too much about the vile living conditions.

The Xinjiang detention camp was completely walled and rectangular in shape with a tall wire fence. The fence had barbed wire on top surrounding the entire camp. I pictured it in my mind like the concentration camps during the holocaust of World War II. All physically able detainees were required to work and produce textile products. Some went into the fields during the day and picked cotton. While others worked in the large warehouse at the camp weaving cotton strands on looms.

Abdulla said that living at the detention camp was like being in a horrifying prison and the conditions were deplorable. She told me that her sister and about twelve other girls were arrested and rounded up one evening on July 15, 2017 and taken to the camp on a bus that had bars on the windows. When they arrived they were taken to a large room and ordered to take off their customary clothes and stand before the guards in their underwear. She said when the girls attempted to cover their bodies with their arms they were slapped or their hair was pulled and they were ordered to put their hands by their sides. If anyone cried they were pulled to the floor by their hair. They were given uniforms and sent to their cells.

Abdulla told me that she quickly learned that all of the girls complained of being beaten and or raped. Then she paused for a good minute and typed I was slapped in the face many times but never beaten like some of the other girls because they didn't want me to look battered so they could promote me to their clients. Then she paused again and put her head down and typed they used me. I knew clearly what she meant by abused and that she must have been raped or had to do things that were against her will. I could see that she was distressed and embarrassed discussing it so I then asked her how long was she in the camp. She said about three months prior to her escape.

She said that all outsiders who came into the camp on business were mean to the detainees except one very nice Chinese couple she met about three months after her confinement. She said she met the couple through Nur who was an older woman detainee who befriended her in camp. Supposedly Nur had been detained in the camp for long time. Nur took her aside and explained how a very nice Chinese couple could help her escape to Turkey for a price. Abdulla said she met with the couple briefly two times and told them that it was okay to discuss the cost of the escape with her parents. She said that her parents were very supportive of her escaping because they did not want her to die in the camp like her younger sister had and that they would do anything and everything they could to get her out or escape. She said that because she was a young Uyghur woman her situation was compounded by the government policy that favored sons over daughters. She said her parents did their best to get her married and that she had a boyfriend. They were planning on getting married but he went missing and she never saw him again. Shortly after he went missing she and her sister were detained and taken to the camp. Abdulla said that it was well known among Uyghur girls that it was much better to be married rather than be unmarried for personal safety reasons.

The Chinese couple met with her parents and a price was agreed. The following evening after the price was agreed to Nur told Abdulla that a plan was in place. Nur explained to Abdulla that she would be transported out of the camp in the back of a delivery van to a very safe area. Abdulla asked where she was going and Nur said again do worry it will be safe and that you will be in Turkey sooner than you think. Then Nur instructed Abdulla that she was to go to the storage room adjacent to the eating area after dinner at precisely six o'clock. She was instructed to wait for the door to the outside to be unlocked. Nur said that the Chinese woman would softly tap on the door two times and Abdulla should listen for the door to be unlocked. She was instructed that when she heard the click of the lock she should then immediately open the door and quickly get into the opened sliding door of the van.

At dinner she kept looking at the large clock high on the wall above the eating area. At six o'clock she got up and casually walked to the storage room. None of the guards made any attempt to stop her. She said her heart was beating so fast she could feel it in her throat and the temples of her head. She approached the door and put her ear against it and listened. She heard the two taps on the door and then the lock clicking and she opened the door and swiftly got into the van. Abdulla asked the Chinese woman where are we going? The Chinese woman told her to be quiet and lie down as the woman covered her with a blanket. Then she could hear the woman move from the back of the van to the front passenger's seat. Before she got under the blanket Abdulla saw the Chinese man in the driver's seat. She held the blanket in place over her body and nervously waited. She thought it was very strange that when the van pulled up to exit the security gate there was no discussion with the guard. Rather she heard the gates open and they simply drove through without any comment.

She said the drive was less than an hour and that they took her to a warehouse in an industrial area. While riding in the back of the van she peeked out from beneath the blanket and saw a slip of paper tucked into the frame of the van wall. The note read "hide". She said it looked like it was written with a rock's edge or dirt. It was faint but clear enough for her to be very concerned. In camp she had heard rumors of girls and women being sold as slaves or forced into the sex trade market, especially pretty girls. She soon realized lying on the floor of the van that the couple wasn't really interested in helping her but rather they were going to sell her in the sex trade market because she was considered by other Uyghur girls in camp to be very pretty.

Walt, this is a very compelling and heartbreaking story but I think you need to be more specific as to how Abdulla got national news media attention. Mrs. Kaster this is why you need to hear the full story. Abdulla never got any news media attention. In fact, no one knows anything about her except me and my parents. If you let me continue you will then have the full story and I am certain that the Bureau would be very interested. Okay, please continue but know that there needs to be something more than what you are currently presenting. I want some specifics about news media involvement. I understand Mrs. Kaster and I will do my best to peak your interest.

It was very dark when the van arrived at the warehouse. When they got out of the van the man turned on his flashlight and aimed it on the padlock that locked the two large aluminum sliding doors. He took off the padlock and slid one of the doors to the left. He shined his flashlight inside as the three of them entered. There was no one inside and the lights were off. She said she was very frightened because of the note that she found in the van that she put in her pant pocket. She then pulled out the folded note from her pocket and gave it to me. But it was illegible because it had been washed with her clothes. But I believed her and then she said that the Chinese couple nicely told her that they were going to lock her inside the warehouse for her own safety and that she should be very quiet. He then shined his flashlight to a large stack of boxes in the back of the warehouse near the bathroom. He told her to hide behind the boxes, to be very quiet and that they would return before sunrise with some food. Then they would leave for their safe journey to Turkey. She said she was very scared and then even more scared when the man firmly instructed her not to make any effort to leave the warehouse because camp security would be looking for her and that if she was caught she would be tortured, raped and then murdered. Then the woman pointed over to the boxes and said go hide now and be quiet. She said she immediately ran over and hid behind the boxes as instructed. The couple exited the warehouse, slid the aluminum door shut and locked it with the padlock. She heard the engine rev on the van and quickly speed away.

She said she knew her life was in danger and that she no longer trusted the couple. She climbed up on top of a box next to the window to look outside. She saw nothing but other similar sized warehouses and determined that trying to escape from the warehouse at that time would most likely result in her being caught. This is when she decided that she had to be smarter than the couple and fool them in thinking she escaped. She climbed down from the box and found a towel in the bathroom and wrapped it around her hand. Then she climbed back up on top of the box and broke the window with her wrapped hand so as to make it look like that she escaped. She then dropped the towel next to the broken glass on the floor of the warehouse. She said the reason she broke the window and left the towel was because she wanted the couple to visibly notice the broken glass and the towel on the floor so they would right immediately conclude that she escaped. But she didn't leave the warehouse and hid in the rafters for two days. At the peak of the warehouse ceiling was a small platform that was used to anchor the rafters. It was big enough and she was small enough for her to lie down and not be seen from the warehouse floor.

The following morning when they came back and saw the broken window with glass and the towel on the warehouse floor they instantly thought she escaped. She said they yelled and screamed at each other for some time. Then they exited the warehouse and she could hear them lock the sliding door. She heard them yelling some more outside and then they sped away. No one else came into the warehouse while she was hiding. She said she waited in the rafters in hopes that she could climb down and then hide in the back of a delivery truck and escape. But no one came. On the second night just before sunset, she climbed down from the rafters and went over to the refrigerator and ate some leftover food and some vegetables. As she was eating she saw in the shipping area of the warehouse a large wooden box. She said that there were multiple urgent shipping labels on the box and that it was being shipped to Los Angeles on Philippine Airlines the following morning. She got a hammer and a screwdriver from a workbench and punched some holes in the box. She said that she removed and hid some of the packages that were in the box to the far side of the warehouse and then climbed into the box and waited. She said that the holes that she made provided enough air to breathe and the box was big enough for her to be able to stretch and curl her legs. Then she said that she was very lucky and surprised because shortly after getting into the box a truck pulled up in front of the warehouse, opened the sliding door, loaded the box into the truck and then took it to Xinjiang airport. She said that within a few hours the box was loaded into the belly of an airplane. While in the air she got out of the box. However she told me that because it was so cold in the belly of the airplane she got back into the box because it was warmer inside during the fourteen hour flight. She said it was freezing cold and she did not know if she would survive but at least she could breathe during the ordeal.

On the fourth day she arrived at LAX and the box was moved to another large warehouse at the airport. She opened the lid of the box that evening and could see that it was safe enough to get out of the box but that there was no place for her to go or hide at the airport. She felt that if she attempted to leave the warehouse area she would be caught and all the pain and suffering she had gone through would have been a wasted effort. She said she went over to the sink and drank lots of water and looked for food but there wasn't any. So she climbed into the back of a large Amazon delivery truck that was completely filled and she hid inside between the boxes. She maneuvered herself between the boxes and found a warm place on the floor that kept her well hidden. That Amazon truck ended up at my Amazon warehouse. Then she said in the early morning it became very quiet in the warehouse and she climbed out of the large Amazon truck and ran across the warehouse to my van and got inside. Inside the van she found one of our empty totes that as I said before are really large soft-sided boxes with a flip top similar to soft-sided picnic coolers. Abdulla was small enough that she was able to hide inside the box. She said that she had not eaten any food for two days until she ate my apples and chips.

Okay Walt, again this is heartbreaking and interesting but you need to cut to the chase and tell me how this all got news media attention and that Abdulla was not the one in the news. I will Mrs. Kaster but please trust me that you need to hear the entire story. I can assure you that what I tell you will also be helpful to your investigation that Agents Michaels and Daniels are conducting. All right Walt, but please note that I must leave at five. I always pick up my daughter after her high school tennis team practice. I cannot be late. I understand Mrs. Kaster and I will do my best to move quickly with the story.

Later in the afternoon we had another long discussion using the computer. I told Abdulla that I had to figure out what to do with her. I explained that that she could not stay with me. She made it quite clear that if I turned her into immigration or the authorities she would be returned to Xinjiang and then executed. She said there was no option for her but to hide and that she would leave whenever I told her to go. I asked her if she knew anyone in the United States and she said no. The only people she knows in the world are in Xinjiang and me.

I told her again she can't stay with me. She never tried to convince me to stay and said that she would leave and hide someplace. I asked her where would she go and she said maybe she could hide in a forest somewhere. I felt so sorry for her and said she could stay with me for one more night. But I said she could not sleep in the bathroom. I told her she had to sleep on the couch or in the bed. She thanked me and said she would sleep on the couch.

Before going to work the next morning I learned that Abdulla not only spoke Uyghur but also Mandarin fluently. Her English was poor but she did understand some basic words. I could now tell that she was intelligent and had more than basic computer knowledge. At the computer she asked me if I had family and I explained that my family lived in another state about five hours away in a place called Las Vegas, Nevada. She said she heard of it and that it was known to her as a city with lots of pretty lights and hotels. I said that I grew up in Las Vegas and that I had only lived in my apartment in Los Angeles for about two months. She asked if there was anything she could do for me while I was at work-like cook or clean. I said no and I got out a map of California and showed her where the nearest forest was located. I don't know why I did this but I didn't know what else to do because I did not want to keep her hiding in my apartment. I had enough of my own problems and I certainly did not want to have any issues with the law given my past. I told her that the forest was less than a two hour drive away and that I would take her there the next morning to the forest, give her some money, some food and a sleeping bag and she could hide. I then paused for a couple of minutes and typed in my computer this is stupid-you can't live in the forest. You can stay with me for a few more days and I will investigate to see if there are any social service agencies or immigration organizations that can help you. She said many times thank you in English.

Before leaving for work I asked her to sit down at the computer with the headphones and learn basic words and sentences in English such as, what time is it, where is the restroom, thank you and goodbye. I said that I don't know is not the best response to questions that are asked of her and it would be good for her to learn some more English. I also told her to eat whatever she wanted. I then asked her to be quiet because I did not want to bring any attention to my apartment. She completely understood.

When I returned in the evening she was sitting at the computer wearing the headphones. She must have been using the computer all day. I motioned to her to come over to the table and eat some soup and bread that I bought at my favorite deli. She said in English thank you. I said syey-syeh in Mandarin and she smiled.

After dinner she had me go over to the computer to learn some basic Mandarin while she cleaned the dishes. This made me laugh out loud and I could see she was very happy. That night she again slept on the couch. I think Abdulla felt very safe with me and it was probably the first time she has felt safe in a long time even though she was not in her own country.

The next morning after breakfast I explained to her using the computer that I had to go to work again and that I might not be back until ten at night. When I got home from work she said in English hello Walt and how are you today. I said hello Abdulla and we both smiled. She had on the table ready for me to eat a kind of pilaf dish that had chicken, carrots and onions. I didn't want to hurt her feelings because I had already eaten but I ate it all and said syey-syeh and she smiled again. Actually, it was quite good and healthier than what I normally eat. She seemed very happy and much more relaxed. I could tell that she felt safe and wanted to stay with me for as long as she could. Before going to bed we went back to the computer and had a lengthy discussion. I explained to her that I had to go back to work in the morning. She said she would have dinner for me again when I got home and I said that would be nice.

I told Abdulla that during my lunch break I would go to the thrift store and buy her some clothes. She smiled and said in English thank you very much Walt. I smiled and it seemed clear to me that we were becoming friends and not me just being her temporary protector.

When I got home from work Abdulla had a pasta soup ready for me that tasted something like minestrone soup and it was very good. I didn't tell her that my efforts to find her help were unproductive. I made several telephone calls while at work to the Center for Human Rights and the American Immigration Council. They both told me that under the Trump administration it would be impossible to find a legal residence for a young Uyghur woman. Further, they said that if Abdulla was found by the United States

Customs or Immigration she would be held in a United States detention camp and then most likely returned to China.

After we ate I gave Abdulla a bag of clothes from the thrift store and she was so excited to try them on. I explained to her that I did not pick out the clothes or the undergarments. I had two reasons for telling her this. One I had no idea what to buy her and two I didn't want to embarrass Abdulla by bringing her under clothes. I told her that I asked the lady at the thrift store to help me buy enough clothes for a few days. I tried to be specific and described Abdulla as a nineteen year old woman, about five foot two inches and probably weighed around 110 pounds. She opened the bag and looked at me and gave me a huge smile and then excitedly ran into the bathroom. First, she modeled her jeans, then calf-length pants and then another pair of jeans. She was very excited about her new clothes. They were so different than what she had been wearing which was simply a red baggy uniform. She looked quite pretty in her new clothes. I felt that if we were to go shopping she would fit in very nicely and would no longer look out of place.

Before going to bed Abdulla came over to me and said to me in English, Walt thank you and then shook my hand. I was very touched by her appreciation and impressed with how much English she had learned. I did not know what to say to her other than you are welcome. She understood me and smiled. She had a beautiful smile with pretty brown eyes.

The next day I had to work. Before going to work I told Abdulla that I would be home about the same time in the evening. When I got home from work she again served the minestrone type soup. I think it was even better than the first time she made it. After we finished dinner she had me cover my eyes. When I opened my eyes she had in front of me a small cake. She said in English honey cake. It was delicious. I learned later that honey cake is made with only three ingredients and that it is quite simple to make but also very popular in Xinjiang.

We sat at the computer for about an hour and communicated about a wide range of things but mostly about her parents and her sister whom she deeply missed. I told her that tomorrow was my day off and we would go shopping for food and anything else she needed. Before we went to bed we made a shopping list.

The next day while at the store a guy that I knew from work came up to me with Abdulla by my side. He said how are you doing Walt and who is this? I said hello Tony and at the same time motioned with my right hand for Abdulla to get some milk. Abdulla knew exactly what I was doing by having her leave so that she would not have to be introduced. I told Tony that Abdulla was a foreign exchange student who was staying with me a couple of days. He said lucky you and I said no it is nothing like that I think she might be gay and that I was helping out a friend by letting her stay in my apartment. Why I said that she might be gay I don't know but it worked.

When Abdulla returned we quickly checked out at the register and drove to the thrift store. On the drive over to the thrift store I dictated into my cell phone again using Google Translate that I told Tony that she was a foreign exchange student living with me for a couple of days. But I didn't tell Abdulla that I said she was gay. At the thrift store she saw the counter with cosmetics and excitedly went over to it and selected several items.

After shopping we went to Taco Bell and we ate in the car. It was the first time she had tacos and she really liked them. That evening we went over to the computer and I explained to her what I learned from the immigration organizations that I contacted. I said that the information was not good. She did not seem the least bit phased by the unfortunate news. I typed aren't you upset? She wrote back no. I didn't think anyone could help Abdulla and that my only alternative for a while was for me to keep her hidden. I wrote you can't stay with me forever. She wrote back I understand and if you can drive me to the forest I will leave in the morning. I paused for a few minutes and wrote you are so brave; in fact, you are the bravest person I know. She wrote I am not brave but I understand the need to think survival. Then I paused again for a longer time and wrote pack up some of your clothes we are going to see my parents in Las Vegas tomorrow and we will be gone two days but only one night because I have to get back to work. She wrote will it be safe? I wrote it will be very safe and my parents might think of some alternatives.

Walt, we are going to need to stop now because as I told you I need to pick up my daughter from her tennis practice. Can you come back tomorrow morning at ten? Yes, and I will see you then.

CHAPTER THREE

VEGAS

Good morning Mrs. Kaster. I think we left off yesterday with me explaining to you how Abdulla escaped from Xinjiang and her living with me in Santa Monica for a few days. So if it is okay I will continue with what happened the next morning. That's fine Walt and please continue with your story.

I had cereal and toast ready for breakfast on the table. Abdulla came out of the bathroom and she looked like a woman and not a teenager. She had put on some lipstick and eye makeup stuff and she looked very attractive-in fact, very pretty. She was obviously familiar with wearing makeup and probably wore it regularly back home in Xinjiang, China. It is not as though Abdulla wasn't pretty without makeup but she just looked more mature, feminine and the makeup accentuated her big beautiful brown eyes. Of course her wearing tight jeans and a pretty blouse made her look a lot more attractive than her baggy red uniform. I said in English that she looked very pretty and she clearly understood. I started to tell her that she looked much shapelier in her jeans than in her red baggy uniform but then I stopped mid-sentence because I thought it might not be appropriate. She didn't understand me but she knew that I thought she looked attractive. While eating breakfast I could not get over how very pretty she looked compared to the scared girl I found in the Amazon box in the back of my van.

On our five hour drive to Las Vegas we practiced English and

Mandarin; but mostly English. She had already learned a great deal on my computer at the apartment and I had learned very little. As we drove I would point at objects such as cars, flowers, mountains, desert, buildings, houses, and etc. and then would say the word in English identifying the object. Abdulla would then point at the object and repeat the word such as mountain in English. She was such a quick learner.

It was about lunchtime and I pulled into a gas station with a diner and asked Abdulla if she wanted to eat something. She said she wasn't very hungry but she would eat a little something if I was hungry. I asked if she would like some dessert. She said why would I eat dessert. Then she pointed out the window to the desert and said we are in the dessert. Then I clarified and asked would you like to eat some dessert. She asked why would I want to eat dessert it looks sandy. I laughed and pointed to the desert and said that is the desert. Desert and dessert sound similar. Then I asked Abdulla if she would like a cookie or pastry. She still did not understand. I said would you like a dessert like the honey cake pastry you made for me in my apartment. She smiled and said yes.

I then asked would you like to go inside the diner. She said I thought you wanted to eat some desert or dessert now and not later. I said I do want to eat now and I pointed to the small restaurant at the gas station and said it is called a diner. I said that the words diner and dinner sound similar but they are different. I explained to her that you can eat dinner in a diner. She looked at me a bit confused and said okay let's go into the dinner or diner and I laughed.

We sat down at a table near the back of the diner. I ordered a hamburger and Abdulla had tea and a doughnut. While we were eating she said she was still confused by the meaning of dinner and diner. I said we are now eating in a diner and that if we were eating in the evening we would be eating dinner in the diner. I am not sure she fully understood but it was fun discussing it. Then she said you have a lot of English words that sound the same. I asked what do you mean? She said the number two has many meanings. She said it means there are two things like the two of us sitting at the table eating together but it can mean also. Don't you think that is funny Walt? I said yes, but they are spelled differently. The number two is spelled t w o and the word too that means also is spelled t o o. She said but they sound the same to me. Then she said there is another funny thing about the number two. I asked what else is funny about the number two. Abdulla said I just said to you that they sound the same to me. To spelled t o is another word that sounds like the number two. I said yes it is also spelled differently and it has another meaning. Then she asked what does it mean? I thought about it for a few seconds and I couldn't think of a good answer. So, I said we needed to finish eating and leave soon so that we can have dinner with my parents at their house and not in a diner. She understood and took another sip of her tea.

Abdulla then said the number two means there is a value of two things like you and me sitting at this table. You are one and I am one which means there are two people. I said Abdulla that is correct. Then she said Walt if I am one and you are one it could mean that we won a prize. I said the number one and the word won sound the same but they have different meanings and they are also spelled differently. Then I explained that the number one is spelled o n e and the word won like winning a prize is spelled w o n. She ate some more of her doughnut as she looked around the diner. A few minutes passed and said you know Walt you ate all of your hamburger and there are eight windows in this diner. I said you are very smart Abdulla and you are also right. English numbers are funny. Then I said we needed to finish eating and that I had to get some gasoline for my car.

We got into the car and I pulled into the gas station island to purchase gas. There was a woman pumping gas at the first pump and I began to pull into the area of the second pump. A guy in a pickup truck swiftly pulled up in front of me from the opposite direction. He made it impossible for me to access the second pump because he blocked the second and third pumps. The woman pumping gas behind me was still pumping gas. My car was at an odd angle and I got out of the car and asked him nicely if he could back up so that I could pump gas at the middle pump. He flipped his cigarette towards me and said no you can wait. I turned and he laughed as I was walking back to my car. I looked at Abdulla and thought I cannot afford to get in a fight with this guy or make a big scene. If I did then the police might be called and it could be very problematic for Abdulla. I looked at Abdulla and she seemed calm but I am sure she wondered why the guy flipped a cigarette at me. I looked at him and couldn't let it go. I felt compelled to ask him again to move his car. I said look, I don't want any trouble I only want gas so please move your truck back a bit so I can pump my gas. He touched my shoulder with his index finger as if he was going to push me away. Then he said you will have to wait for me to pump my gas or you can go on the other side of the island and pump gas. I moved up closer to him and he stepped back and then I said I don't think so. He said what do you mean you don't think so? I said you made two mistakes. One, you touched me and two that is one ugly baseball cap you are wearing. Then I said you have me blocked in and I think you are more fluff than stuff so move your truck back now or there will be trouble. He looked at me and saw the woman pumping gas behind my car. We both could tell that she was alarmed and that she thought something bad was about to happen between us. But it didn't and he got in his truck without pumping gas, backed up and sped away.

I got in my car to move it forward and Abdulla immediately asked what I talked to the man about. I said I asked him to move his truck because he was blocking the gas pump and he decided to leave. She said I heard you say to him that he was more fluff than stuff. Then she asked me what that meant. I said do you know what a marshmallow looks like? She said yes. I said if you look at a marshmallow it looks like it could be hard and tough but when you touch it you learn that it is soft. I then explained that the guy with the truck was trying to be tough with me but he was soft. Abdulla said nothing but she clearly understood. I filled the gas tank and we continued our drive.

During our drive, she pointed at the far off snow capped Sierra Mountain range and said to me in English home. I knew then that where she lived in Xinjiang there must have been snow capped mountains with a forest. Then she pointed at the forest and said in English the forest is not far. She must have memorized this while using my computer when she thought she was going to need to hide in the forest after staying with me in Santa Monica. I realized then that in her village some Uyghurs must have hidden in the forest to escape detention. I also understood why she suggested to me the first day we met that she could hide in the forest. After learning about all she endured in that detention camp and her escape there was no way I would ever let her hide in the forest.

I was impressed with how much English she had learned in her four days with me. In fact, just prior to arriving in Las Vegas she said to me in English where is the restroom? We then stopped at a gas station and went inside to use the restroom. As we left the gas station she said to the man behind the counter quite clearly in English thank you and he said you are welcome. Obviously, with her broken English and hand gestures, Abdulla was beginning to be able to partake in basic conversational English. I on the other hand was not much better at speaking Mandarin than when we left my apartment.

When we got to my parents home I introduced Abdulla to them and they were both very welcoming. I said Abdulla this is my

Mom Marian and my father Peter. I could tell that my Mom wanted to hug her but did not because none of us knew if it was appropriate. We sat on the couch in their living room and I explained to them in detail how I found Abdulla in the back of my van and how she escaped from a detention camp in Xinjiang. I attempted to repeat everything I learned from Abdulla about her detention and escape. Both of them listened intently and my Mom's eyes started to tear. She got up and said you both must be thirsty and she went into the kitchen. I asked my Dad in front of Abdulla what should I do? I explained that she said she would hide in the forest like some of her villagers did in Xinjiang but that there was no way I would let that happen. Abdulla understood some very basic conversational English but I was certain she did not comprehend his response. She sat there quietly on the couch and my Dad said I had three alternatives. One, apply for asylum knowing that President Trumps anti Muslim immigration policy would most likely result in Abdulla being returned to Xinjiang, China. He said if she filed for asylum she would probably end up in a United States detention camp and held for an extended period of time and then most likely returned to China. Two, find her an illegal job and let her fend for herself. And three, marry her or find someone else to marry her so as to help get her a visa or a green card and then she can ultimately apply for citizenship. But he said marriage was no guarantee because he thought there were strict regulations governing marriage of illegal immigrants. I liked Abdulla very much but not in a romantic way and I said dad that's not going to happen. I certainly thought Abdulla was very nice, pretty and needed help because of her circumstances but I was not interested in marriage. So I said that this was out of the question.

After my Mom brought in some water and tea the four of us sat down at their computer and I wrote on Google Translate Abdulla you have two options. I did not include marriage as an option. However, I think she already knew because in China Uyghur girls and women must have discussed openly all their options about immigration matters. I explained each option and then told Abdulla that I thought her best option was to find her own place to live and look for work. It was already translated on the screen and my Mom put her hand on mine over the computer mouse and said tell her she can stay with us while she looks for work here in Vegas. My Dad said what? Abdulla did not know what the three of us were talking about. Then my Mom said we have two spare rooms and we have to help her. She said Abdulla can use one of the rooms until she gets enough money to have her own place. My Mom moved me away from the computer and typed Abdulla you can stay with us and find work. Abdulla's face lit up with happiness and she got up from her chair and hugged my Mom as my Mom sat in front of the computer. This is the first time Abdulla physically touched anyone in the United States except when she shook my hand in my apartment after I gave her a bag of clothes from the thrift store a couple of days ago. I remember her saying in English as she shook my hand thank you Walt. However, she touched all of us emotionally after learning about the deplorable life that she had to endure in China and the life threatening experience coming to the United States.

After dinner, I took Abdulla for a walk on the Strip and she was amazed at all the lights as is everyone who visits Las Vegas for the first time. As we walked on the Strip Abdulla practiced her English pointing at objects and then telling me what they were. She even said fountain in front of Caesars Palace. I did not talk much but rather just listened to her speak with her soft sounding voice and accent as she pointed at objects and repeated in English what they were. I could tell from her demeanor that she felt very safe with me even though there were so many people walking the streets late at night.

In the morning after breakfast with my small duffel bag in hand, I explained to Abdulla that I had to leave and return home and go back to work. Although she did not understand the words I was speaking she understood and said to me as I was going out the front door in English thank you very much Walt. Then she said in almost perfect English I appreciate everything you did for me and I will repay you for the clothes. She must have practiced this many times on the computer while staying at my apartment so that she could say it to me at the proper time. I shook my head many times indicating no and the only words I could think of were syey-syeh. She smiled and knew that I did not want her to repay me for anything. I then opened my wallet and gave her $40. She said no and I insisted and then I left. I think I felt a little sad about leaving her.

A few days later my Mom telephoned me and told me that prior to Abdulla being detained she was a grade school teacher in Xinjiang teaching young children how to use computers. She also said that she thought Abdulla was very smart and that she was quickly learning more English and becoming more fluent. I know that my Mom was really enjoying having Abdulla live at the house and my Dad liked it as well. She helped my Mom with house cleaning and chores and as they were doing things together they were both learning one another's language.

Then my Mom explained to me in detail what Abdulla told her about the horrific conditions while she lived in the detention camp in Xinjiang.

Walt let's break for lunch and I will see you again at one-thirty.

CHAPTER FOUR

THE CAMP

I remember the day so clearly. It was a warm day at my school, in fact, it was so warm we had to have all the windows opened in my Xinjiang classroom. That day some of the children came to school very stressed and frightened because there was another roundup the prior evening of children being taken to an Education Training Center. Marian, these Centers are nothing more than internment camps with the goal of reprogramming young Uyghur children to expunge their customs, heritage and Muslim religion. I was of course concerned about how distressed these little sweet children were and so I had them sing happy uplifting songs in hopes of reducing their stress before starting their computer lessons. I was a teacher at the school and my specialty was to introduce children to using computers. I loved my job teaching and working with these beautiful innocent children. I was also in training to be a full time teacher at the school and I only had five months to go before being advanced to a permanent teacher position.

Everyone in our village was distressed about these abductions. However, there was nothing we could do except hope and pray that it would stop soon. Sometimes several weeks or even months would pass between abductions. At dinner that night my parents, my sister Patime and I talked about the abductions of the children the night before and the pain that the families must be going through worrying about their children. We again talked about how we could escape to Turkey but our discussions were nothing more than hope because it was impossible to leave. Any effort to leave would result in imprisonment or detention in a camp.

Teenagers and adults were also detained in camps but these camps were not only reprogramming camps but labor camps and the conditions were known to be horrid. Detainees worked long hours in the fields or in warehouses producing textiles. On July 15, 2017 a government bus with about a dozen other Uyghur young women pulled up to our home. Several guards got out of the bus and forced my sister and me to get in the bus. Patime cried and screamed fighting with the guards not to get into the bus. One of the guards pulled her by the hair to the ground and then dragged her into the bus. I could see some of Patime's beautiful black hair on the ground. I attempted to help Patime but was kicked in the leg and then I fell to the ground in extreme pain. The guard then kicked me in the stomach and told me to get into the bus which I did even though the pain in my leg and stomach was unbearable. But I did not want to be further injured. Our parents could do nothing but let them take us away and hope that we would not be further injured.

When we arrived at the camp I could see that it was a huge fenced rectangular prison. The fencing was very tall with barbed wire on top surrounding the camp. It seemed clear to me that once inside the camp there was no way to escape. We got off the bus and went into an eating area. We were then served food even though it was in the late evening. It was actually decent and some of us then thought that maybe being detained in the camp would not be as bad as the stories we heard in our village about the horrid camp conditions.

After we ate everything changed for the worse. We were told to line up and remove our customary clothes, shoes and jewelry and strip down to our underwear. Patime said she wouldn't do it. A guard came up to her and slapped her in the face and then she started crying. I told Patime to stop crying and do as told and she was slapped again. She stopped crying and whimpered as she got undressed. It was so embarrassing and frightening. One young woman could not handle the embarrassment and started crying uncontrollably. Two guards came up to her and one slapped her face and the other stood behind her and hit her in the back of the head with the palm of his hand. She bent over crying and the guard who was behind her pulled her by the hair to make her stand up straight. She stood up and her crying began to subside. Patime was still whimpering. A guard walked up close to her and then again slapped her in the face. He said stop crying and she did.

We were then instructed to pick up our clothes. For some unknown reason which I never understood we were instructed to remove all elastic and buttons from our clothes and put them in a pile in a bowl on the floor in front of us.

Abdulla, let me type now, please. I can see the pain in your face as you are typing on my computer about the awful conditions you endured at the detention camp. Do you want to take a break or tell me about it another time? No, Marian it will do me good to tell you about it and you are the only one in the world that I can discuss this with. Okay, Abdulla if you are sure you want to continue please continue.

We stood there undressed for about five minutes as the guards eyed us up and down making sure we were not hiding anything like valuables or jewelry. When any of the young women attempted to cover their bodies with their arms they were slapped in the face or their hair was pulled. We were all ordered to keep our hands down by our sides. If anyone cried they were slapped or pulled to the floor by their hair. After the guards were sure we did not have anything hidden a guard came into the eating area with a cart and gave us our red uniforms. We were then escorted to our cells.

Each cell was home to fourteen women, with bunk beds, bars on the windows, a basin and a hole-in-the-floor-style toilet. Everyone got along because we all knew that we had to work together to survive and that any complaining or discontent exhibited would result in being beaten by the guards.

Everyone was required to work producing textile products. Some went into the fields during the day and picked cotton. While others worked in the large warehouse at the camp weaving cotton strands on looms. We all learned very quickly that if we complained we would be taken away and beaten and or raped. When this happened and a girl or woman returned to her cell she would say nothing about what transpired but we could all see the signs of her being beaten and abused. Sometimes we could see hair missing from the head, bruises and scratches on the face and dark bruises on the wrist from being handcuffed.

I remember one time a girl who was working on a loom machine next to me began to feel very weak and faint. A guard yelled at her and we all watched to see what was going to happen. She was pulled on the back of her collar to the floor and told by the guard to get in the "motorcycle position" if you are tired and want to rest. The motorcycle position is not painful at first but as time passes it is very uncomfortable or even painful. The way it is done is the detainee squats on the floor and stretches her two arms out front of her as far as she can and at the same time the knees are bent in a half-squat position. Sometimes the detainee has to hold the position for five minutes which can be painful. If a detainee does not hold in position as instructed then they would get hit or kicked. At one time I was kicked in the abdomen for not holding in the motorcycle position long enough as ordered and I fell to the floor and passed out. That night I was bleeding from my private area and one of my cellmates called for a guard. A guard took me to the dispensary and I was held there for two nights. When I returned to my cell all the women were told by the guard that "don't you know that all women bleed" implying that what I experienced was normal.

When I returned my sister Patime was not in the cell. I asked some of the women where is my sister? But no one answered. Nur, an older woman in the cellblock who befriended me, came into our cell and said that Patime had some intestinal issues and was sent to another dispensary. Three days later I was told by Nur that Patime died of a mysterious illness. I never saw my sweet sister Patime again who I thought lost her life at only fifteen years old. I hoped that she was still alive and that maybe she was taken to another camp because she complained so much about the conditions. But my parents later confirmed that Patime actually died in camp and that they buried her but did not know what caused her death.

Some of the detainees who had been there for several months were so thin that you could see the outline of their bones in their faces and arms. Many of them had lost their hair due to poor diet and stress and some had their heads shaved. After about three weeks in camp all I could think about was wishing I had a full stomach. We were all so hungry and missing our customary food.

We all had to participate in classes learning Mandarin, singing for hours in Mandarin patriotic Chinese songs, watching patriotic TV programs and memorizing patriotic propaganda about our supposedly superior Chinese Communist Party form of government. We were told that the government needed to wash our brains, cleanse our hearts, strengthen our righteousness and eliminate the evil within us. One quickly forgets what life is like outside the camp and you begin to wonder if the brainwashing is working or if it is the side effect of injections and pills. All the women in my cell were given some form of mandatory birth control. At least we thought the injections or pills were used to control birth. Marian, you are probably wondering why they would want us to be on birth control if we were always around other women in our cell block and there was no escape. The answer is simple. There was an organized program of rape in our camp.

During the first few weeks we heard stories of women being taken out of their cells at night and being moved. When this happened it meant they were being moved closer to the "black room". The black room was a place where women were beaten and raped but mostly raped.

All the guards wore masks to hide their faces. No one else wore masks and the flu season was over. Some of the guards wore suits and some wore uniforms. Almost all wore hats. I could never tell if men wearing suits were supervisors, guards or outsiders. It didn't make any difference what they wore because they all wore a mask. We were all frightened every night of the week that we might be taken to the black room. When this happened it usually would take place sometime after midnight. Guards or men in suits wearing masks would come into our cells and select the young women they wanted to rape. They would be forcibly removed from their cell and slapped as they walked down the outer corridor hall of the black room if they complained. Surveillance cameras were everywhere in camp except near the black room and its corridor. We could hear the screams coming from the black room.

It is so hard for me to tell you Marian but I was raped three times during my three months in camp and I had to perform sexual acts that were unthinkable to me. I am scarred for life. I have regular nightmares reliving the horror in that camp. It makes it difficult and sometimes impossible for me to sleep. However, I was one of the lucky ones because I was not beaten or gang-raped. I was slapped a lot but not beaten. I was always raped by men in suits and I assumed they were not guards but rather outsiders who paid. I have no proof that they paid. I soon learned that the reason I was not beaten or gang-raped was because I was considered one of the prettiest inmates and they did not want to damage their "product". It is because of this that I was only raped three times. Some of the women in my cell were raped many times or gang-raped while being handcuffed. Many women had brown markings or scars on their wrists from the handcuffs. Gang-rape was not uncommon and handcuffs were regularly used.

All outsiders who came into the camp on business were mean to the detainees except one day I met a Chinese couple that I thought was nice. I was introduced to them through Nur who was the older woman I told you about. She befriended me a few weeks after arriving at the camp. After meeting with the Chinese couple I felt I could trust them. I agreed to have them meet with my parents to secure payment for my escape to Turkey. Most of us believed that Turkey was one of the better places for Uyghurs to seek asylum. I am not sure that is true. After one short meeting with my parents, a price was agreed. But Marian, the Chinese couple only wanted to sell me as a sex slave or place me in a sex trafficking business. I have given it a lot of thought and I now think Nur was also part of the plan and she was not really my friend.

Marian, you now know everything including my escape to Los Angeles and how Walt saved me in his Amazon van. I hope you don't think less of me.

Abdulla stop and say no more. I do not think anything less of you. In fact, I think you are a very strong woman and one who should be admired. I am so proud of you and happy that you are living with us. I insist that we get up from our chairs and get away from this computer and go for a long walk. What you endured was horrific and I am sorry that you had to experience such horror.

CHAPTER FIVE

RICARDO

How was your lunch Walt? I ate in your downstairs cafeteria and it wasn't bad. Walt, again I want to restate that we have as much time as you need. So, please continue where you left off before lunch. I think Mrs. Kaster we left of when I was telling you that I took Abdulla to my parents' house in Las Vegas and that she is now living with them. Yes, I think that is correct so please continue.

I got routine telephone reports from my Mom about how Abdulla was adapting to her new environment in Las Vegas. About two months passed since Abdulla moved in with my parents and my Mom telephoned me and sounded absolutely frantic. I asked my Mom what was wrong and she said that she thought Abdulla could be getting into trouble. I asked what kind of trouble? She said Abdulla has made several female friends at work. However, she does not socialize with them outside of work because they are also illegal and none of them want to get caught by immigration. She said that Abdulla has a male friend that my parents don't like him at all. They are concerned because Abdulla has started dating him. My Mom said your Dad and I don't like this Ricardo guy and we don't trust him. We think he is up to no good. Then she said that she thinks he sells drugs or does something illegal because he has an expensive car and he wears pricey clothes. She also said that she has seen him at the supermarket a couple of times with two of his friends and they looked very seedy to her.

Walt, it is now four-thirty and I must leave at five. As I explained earlier I always pick up my daughter up after school and I cannot be late. I will do my best to move more quickly and explain to you what transpired that got nationwide news media attention. However, if the Bureau is going to hire me I need to be totally truthful with you and not hide any information. You need to know everything that happened because none of the federal, state or local police agencies including the Las Vegas Criminal Court knows the whole truth.

My Mom said that Abdulla's three female friends were not only illegal but young and each had financial problems. She said one of them was from San Salvador who she thought was about sixteen years old. She said that the other two from Cuba and India looked a little older. All three of them could speak some English and so they were able to communicate with Abdulla to some extent and share their stories about how they illegally entered the United States. Abdulla told me that her three friends reside in shared homes with other illegal young women and that they all worry about being picked up by Immigration. She told my Mom that she feels so fortunate to be living with my parents in a safe, comfortable and loving place while her friends are in constant fear of being caught by Immigration and having to live in meager crowded housing conditions.

Supposedly, Ricardo has lots of money to spend and my parents were sure he was up to no good. I asked my Mom what does Abdulla say about him. She said that he takes her to nice restaurants and that she loves to go to the movies with him. He even buys her some clothes. I asked my Mom why she didn't just tell Abdulla not to date him anymore. She said that Abdulla felt safe with him and he treats her like a woman and not like a peasant or a poor immigrant like some of the men do at APEX Farming.

Abdulla explained to my Mom that she thought he must be a hard worker because he has a lot of money and she didn't think that there was anything wrong with being his friend. I told my Mom that I would drive to Vegas on the weekend and look into it. Then I asked her to get me his car license plate number so that I could check him out. This is when things began to escalate and ultimately get out of control.

I arrived in Vegas around noon and only my Dad was home. My Dad basically said the same thing that my Mom told me on the phone about how she did not trust Ricardo. He said the both of them were quite worried about Abdulla dating Ricardo. They also were very concerned about her safety and being picked up by immigration. But they felt they could not do anything to stop Abdulla from seeing Ricardo because they worked together at APEX Farming. Then my Dad said you know she is old enough to make adult decisions, she turned twenty years old last weekend. However, they were both very concerned that she might be manipulated into doing something illegal and that Immigration would eventually find Abdulla.

I asked my Dad where my Mom and Abdulla were. He said they went grocery shopping and they love to be together. He said that they talk constantly and Abdulla's English is so improved from when she first moved to Las Vegas.

My Dad and I talked some more and I learned that Abdulla was working Monday through Friday in the warehouse at APEX Farming. It appears that APEX Farming has a loose employment policy and knowingly hires illegal workers. Abdulla started in the fields but within a couple of days she was moved inside the warehouse doing packing and odd jobs in the main office for the foreman and the supervisors. She said some of the men in the warehouse flirt with her and she didn't like it all. But she said they never touched her. She also said that she thinks she may have gotten moved inside the warehouse because they thought she was pretty and that this is where she met Ricardo.

What I am about to tell you Mrs. Kaster is very important. Abdulla told my Dad that the warehouse has a large packing area downstairs with two small offices. One of the offices is for the foreman and the other office is for the two supervisors. Ricardo also works inside the warehouse but he has a larger private office upstairs on a large loft that is reached by climbing a long staircase on the opposite side of the warehouse that looks down on the two offices below. Abdulla explained to my Dad that there were no other offices upstairs and Ricardo's office had big glass windows but the blinds were always closed and never opened. She said no one ever went inside his office other than Ricardo and that she had never been inside his office. She told my Dad that she did not know what Ricardo did but that she thought he was in some form of sales. She asked him one time what kind of work did he do and his answer was I am on the phone all the time. He never told her what he actually did but she always assumed he was in sales

About an hour later my Mom and Abdulla came home from shopping and my Mom gave me a big hug. She seemed so happy and relieved that I was home because she was concerned about Abdulla's safety and her dating Ricardo. Abdulla and I smiled at each other and said hello but we did not touch. She looked very attractive and so much more confident than when she briefly lived with me in Santa Monica. She said in English how are you Walt and it is very nice to see you. I said Happy Birthday Abdulla and I handed her a wrapped present. She smiled, sat down on the couch, unwrapped the ribbon from the box and opened it. She said thank you very much Walt and then put on the bracelet. She was so happy that it made us all smile and laugh. She then asked me how I was doing. I said all was good with me and I would like to take her to lunch at McDonald's. She smiled and said yes. Her English was getting so much better and her soft accent was so comforting for me to listen to.

At McDonald's Abdulla said she remembered when I took her to the one near the airport after finding her in the back of my Amazon van in the red box. She said she recalled how hungry she was and how badly she needed to use the restroom. As we talked I could hardly believe how well her English had improved and how quickly she had learned. We both laughed and for the first time I realized how pretty she was with her big brown eyes and beautiful smile that would light up any room. We ate lunch and I learned about her job, her three friends and Ricardo. I did not tell her why I was visiting but I did my best to learn everything I could about her job and Ricardo. She said Ricardo isn't really my boyfriend but we have a lot of fun together and he treats me very nicely. Then she said he makes a lot of money at APEX, takes her to nice restaurants and that she feels safe with him. I think for some reason I felt a little envious or possibly even jealous. I asked Abdulla what kind of work Ricardo did at APEX Farming. Abdulla said she wasn't quite sure but she thought he was in some kind of sales work, that he has a big office upstairs in the warehouse and that he is on the phone all day.

Abdulla did not know that my Mom called me expressing her concern about her dating Ricardo or that I got his car license number. After getting his license number it was quite easy for me to learn that his last name is Sanchez and that he lives in one of the Artesian Luxury Apartments not far from the Las Vegas strip.

That night my Mom made a nice pasta dinner. After dinner I explained to my parents and Abdulla that I was going to visit an old friend that I had not seen for a while. Abdulla looked very disappointed. In fact, I think she was very upset with me. I think she thought I would spend more time with her and that my leaving to see a friend was very disappointing. I said goodbye and then drove to Ricardo's apartment.

It was only seven in the evening and I had no idea if I would be able to track down Ricardo. But I did have his address and apartment number at the Artesian Luxury Apartments. I found his car right away parked in front of his apartment. I parked directly across the street from his parked black Mercedes-Benz S Class C. It was not even a year old. I knew from my prior employment working for the Las Vegas Police Department that the Mercedes-Benz S Class C four door model was one of Mercedes-Benz high-end luxury vehicles. I thought it was unlikely that someone working in a warehouse at APEX Farming could afford such a car.

I sat in my car waiting for Ricardo to come out to his car. I was prepared to wait as long as needed. I lucked out because at about seven-thirty a guy who I thought might be Ricardo came out of the Artesian Luxury Apartment building alone and got into the Mercedes. I had no idea if it was Ricardo because I didn't know what he looked like. I only knew the car that he drove. He started his car and drove off and I followed him. He first stopped at Aurora Luxury Apartments and picked up two very attractive young women. Both were dressed in very tight short dresses and stiletto type heels. One of the women looked like she was from India and the other from Asia. In any event they were both drop dead beautiful. I assumed that they were hookers but on the other hand lots of women vacationing in Las Vegas look like that so I didn't really know. They drove off and I followed them to the entrance of Caesars Palace Hotel and Casino. The three of them got out of the car and Ricardo went over to one of the attendants near the front door entrance and said something to him in his ear. He then tipped him. The two women followed the attendant inside the hotel and Ricardo got back into his car and drove to the Bellagio Hotel and parked in the large circular driveway near the entrance. He then got out of his car and went over to one of the attendants and said something to him and gave him a tip. He then got back into his car and waited. About fifteen minutes passed and an absolutely beautiful young tall Asian woman with very long black hair walked out the front door of the hotel and got into his Mercedes. She looked very young and also looked like a hooker. But who can tell because women dress so seductively now and on the strip and it is more common than uncommon. I then suspected that Ricardo was a pimp or involved in some kind of sex trafficking because all the women so far that I had seen with him were obviously young, very pretty and ethnic.

I followed him again and Ricardo dropped the beautiful young Asian woman off at a mansion in the Ridges neighborhood which is a luxury complex of homes for the wealthy. This is when I thought Ricardo was involved in illegal organized prostitution or sex trafficking in Las Vegas.

It was about ten and I then followed him to a major strip club just off the strip. He went inside and I got out of my car and I followed. I had to pay the cover charge and order a drink in order to stay inside the club. When I sat down inside the bar I could not see Ricardo anywhere so I watched the strippers and waited. One of the things that struck me about the girls dancing was that they were all distinctly from various ethnic groups. There were no white or black girls dancing at least while I was there. They were all pretty and young just like Abdulla. I suspected that Ricardo might be using these women's illegal status as leverage to get them to participate in stripping and prostitution. However, the truth of the matter is I wasn't really sure the guy I was following was Ricardo.

I drank another beer, looked around for Ricardo and I waited. About an hour passed and the guy I thought I was following came out from a back room with two other guys. I didn't know if it was Ricardo or not. I got up from my bar stool and walked over to where Ricardo was standing and talking to two guys from the strip club. As I edged up closer I could hear him joking with the two guys. Then one of the guys said Ricardo, no more booze tonight, you don't want to get stopped again by the cops. I then knew this guy I had been following was for certain Ricardo.

He left the club and returned to the Bellagio Hotel. He pulled up in front of the hotel, got out of his car and then tipped one of the attendants. The attendant made a telephone call and about ten minutes later a very young attractive tall Asian woman got into his car.

I had seen enough and I drove back to my parents' house and when I opened the front door I could see Abdulla waiting for me in the kitchen. I asked her why she was still awake at almost two in the morning. She said I wanted to talk to you because I thought we were friends and you would want to see me during your short visit here in Las Vegas. I explained that I did very much want to visit with her but that I had to see my friend and I would talk to her in the morning. She asked me if we could talk now and I said I needed to get some sleep. Actually, I wasn't that tired but I wasn't sure how I was going to tell her about her friend Ricardo. She was obviously very disappointed with me. She said nothing more, got up from the kitchen table and went into her bedroom visibly upset.

I overslept and went into the kitchen in the late morning. I asked my Mom and Dad where Abdulla was and they said that Ricardo already picked her up and that they would be back in a few hours. I told my parents what I had learned the night before about Ricardo and that I was certain he was involved in prostitution and possibly sex trafficking. I told them that I suspected that all the young women he was with the prior night and transporting to various hotels were illegally here and most likely were prostitutes. They were not surprised and asked me if I was going to tell Abdulla. I said I would tell her as soon as she gets home. I anxiously awaited her return.

Two hours did not pass but rather five hours and I was very concerned about Abdulla's safety. When she returned home and came in the front door she was obviously very happy. She looked very pretty dressed up in high heels and wearing an elegant wrap-around type dress. I told Abdulla that she looked very nice and that I needed to talk to her right away. She said she didn't want to talk now but would rather talk later. I wondered if she was trying to get back at me for allegedly visiting my friend last night and not visiting her. I said Abdulla I need to talk to you about something very important right now. She said maybe later. I said no Abdulla we need to talk now. She said she did not want to talk. I then knew she was trying to get back at me for not being with her the prior night. I said that I have something very important and it cannot wait. Abdulla then said I have never seen you be so forceful with me and you are always so polite, but now you seem so bossy. I apologized but I said I had a very good reason. She said she was going to use the bathroom and change her clothes and then she would talk with me in the back yard.

Sitting at the picnic table outside I wondered how I was going to tell Abdulla that Ricardo was not to be trusted. She walked down the back steps of the kitchen and she looked beautiful. I said Abdulla please sit down, I have something very important to tell you. She smiled and said sure but what is so important. I said do you remember when you told me about the nice Chinese couple you met in Xinjiang that you trusted? She said of course I do. I should have never trusted them or Nur because they wanted to sell me as a prostitute or as a sex slave. I said you are not going to like what I am about to tell you but your friend Ricardo is in a similar business and I am positive that he cannot be trusted. She asked me what I meant. I fully explained to her why I was out late the prior night and what I had learned about Ricardo. I was very specific about my following him to hotels and strip clubs. She said she was very surprised and that she always felt safe with him. But she said looking directly into my eyes that she felt safer with me and she knew that I could always be trusted. Then she said she always trusted me more than Ricardo. I didn't know for sure but I think she also meant she liked me more than Ricardo.

As we sat at the picnic table I learned more about her friends and how frightened they were about being caught by Immigration. But I also learned from Abdulla that her friends also felt safe around Ricardo and that they thought he would do his best to protect them from Immigration officers. She said that he told her once he has connections with Immigration. Then Abdulla said the reason she was all dressed up earlier was because Ricardo was going to help her get work at a modeling agency that specialized in ethnic clothing. She said he took her to an office this morning where she met two men. They had a very brief interview and she modeled the dress she was wearing earlier. I explained that I suspected they were the same two men that I saw at the strip club last night. I then told Abdulla that I thought she was being groomed to work at the same strip club and possibly later as a prostitute. Abdulla then said it was a mistake for her to trust Ricardo and he was probably no different than the Chinese couple and Nur that were supposedly going to help her escape from the detention camp in Xinjiang.

We sat at the picnic table quietly for a few minutes and then I said that she could no longer live in Las Vegas. I said Abdulla you have to leave. I explained that I was concerned for her welfare and that I was certain that Ricardo would use her illegal immigration status as leverage to keep her under his control. I told her that if she stayed in Las Vegas then Ricardo at some point soon would make her work at a strip club and ultimately later work as a prostitute. I explained that I was certain he would use her illegal status to coerce her to do things she did not want to do. Then I told her I would not let that happen to her under any circumstance. Abdulla got up from the picnic table and came over to my side of the table and sat down next to me. Then she picked up my hand and held it tightly. It felt very good to me and I felt an emotional relief of some kind that I did not understand then. But I understand it now. I knew then that I had feelings for Abdulla and I was probably more jealous of Ricardo than envious when Abdulla said she trusted him.

We sat there quietly at the picnic table for a few minutes. I then took her hand and looked straight into her eyes and said Abdulla if Ricardo finds out that you know about the kind of evil work he is involved in then he will threaten you with turning you in to immigration. I told Abdulla that she needs to telephone Ricardo right away and tell him that she is moving to San Francisco to help a very sick friend and that she needs to quit her job at APEX Farming. She got up from the picnic table, went inside, telephoned Ricardo and left a voice message. I told Abdulla that we would leave first thing in the morning and that she could stay with me in Santa Monica until we found another safe place for her to live.

This is an incredible story Walt and it would make a good book but I need to know about the shooting and what happened to Abdulla. It is nearing five and I have to leave for the day. How about coming back tomorrow at ten in the morning? Sure that works for me and I will see you then.

CHAPTER SIX

THE CONFLICT

You are right on time again Walt and I appreciate your punctuality. Did you eat breakfast in the cafeteria? I didn't have time for breakfast because I had a dental appointment with my favorite dentist Dr. Fung. But I did have a bag of peanuts on my drive to your office. Are you ready to continue with your interview? Yes I am Mrs. Kaster.

You were telling me Walt that Abdulla left a telephone message with Ricardo that she was quitting APEX Farming under the pretense that she needed to move to San Francisco to help a friend who was ill. Did I get that right? Yes, Mrs. Kaster you are a very good listener. Walt, you have a very interesting story and I am taking notes so it is not difficult to recall where we left off. Please continue with your story.

At about 8:00 that night I was in the bathroom shaving and I heard the doorbell ring. I stepped away from the sink and stood in the bathroom doorway with my razor in my hand and watched my Dad answer the front door. It was Ricardo. He said that he wanted to see Abdulla. My Dad nicely told him that she was sleeping and for him to come back tomorrow. Ricardo said I know she's not sleeping because when I pulled up in the driveway I could see through the window the three of you in the kitchen. My Dad said nicely that's true but you can't see her now because it's getting late. Ricardo said it is only eight o'clock. Then my Dad said that is also true but Abdulla has had a hard long day and she needs to get her rest. Then Ricardo said I don't think so because I was with her part of the day and she wasn't working. Then he said I want to see Abdulla now. I walked up closer to the back of the front door as my Dad firmly said you can't see her as I intently listened. Ricardo did not know I was standing behind the door but my Dad did. Then Ricardo angrily said look old man, I want to see her now. My Dad kept his composure and calmly but confidently said you can't see Abdulla. Then more angrily Ricardo said you don't want to fuck with me old man. My Dad interrupted him and firmly and forcefully said maybe you don't want to fuck with me and get the hell off my front porch. Then Ricardo yelled back this is going to go bad for you old man and then I opened the door all the way as my Dad stepped aside. He said who are you? I said I am his son and a friend of Abdulla's. Then I said Ricardo I think you need to leave now. He said listen friend, if you don't want trouble then you better go get Abdulla and bring her to me now. I said Ricardo I am not your friend and you don't know me. Ricardo said I know you got balls like your old man and if you don't bring me Abdulla things are going to go very bad for you both. Then Ricardo said how do you know my name? I said because I know something about pimps in Las Vegas. He said what makes you think I am a pimp you shithead? I sidestepped answering him because I really didn't know much about Las Vegas pimps. However, I knew he was one and I wanted to get his attention that I knew something about him. Then I said do you know who lives in the Artesian Luxury Apartments off the Strip? Ricardo said no. Then I said I do. Then Ricardo said with a surprised look on his face, you do? Then I said staring directly into his eyes, no Ricardo I know who lives there and it is you. Then Ricardo said how do you know I live at the Artesian? I said because I have been following you and I know what you do and I know you are a Vegas pimp and involved in other bad shit. He stood there angrily looking at me thinking about what he was going to do next. I said firmly but also nicely Ricardo it is time for you to go. He said you don't want to fuck with me asshole. I then said I think you got it wrong Ricardo; you should be the one that doesn't want to fuck with me. Then I stepped a bit closer to him and he did not move back. So, I knew he was not afraid of me. I said do you remember the rookie Las Vegas police officer who was discharged from the police department a while back and jailed a couple of years ago for using excessive force? He said no and I don't give a shit. I said Ricardo you have a way with words and now I know you are dumber than you look. He seemed a bit perplexed by my insult which clearly irked him and made him even angrier. I didn't care because I had fire in my belly and I wanted him to think I was in charge of the situation and not him. He then stepped back a little and yelled at me and said go get Abdulla. I said Ricardo you really don't know me and I am one that should not be ordered. So I will tell you why you should leave. When I got fired from the Las Vegas Police Department it was in all the local newspapers. He said I don't give a shit and you better get out of my way because I am coming in like it or not. I interrupted him again and said no, you're not coming in. Then I said it appears that both the police department and the court seem to think that I overreacted when I brutally beat up a husband who had severely battered his wife during a domestic dispute. Then I lost my jòb with the Las Vegas Police Department and was jailed for a while. If needed I will go to jail again for as long as I have to for my family and my friend Abdulla. I then said calmly and firmly, Ricardo you need to listen to me very carefully. During the domestic dispute the husband attacked me and pulled my firearm and I almost lost control of it. A police officer is to never lose control of his firearm and no one ever pulls a gun on me without repercussions. You do know what repercussion means-don't you? Let me explain it to you in case the word is too big for you. Repercussion means consequence. If consequence is still too big of a word for you to understand it means aftermath. In other words, some type of negative outcome will occur. Any way during my Department's Internal Affairs hearing I was questioned repeatedly why I used extreme force to control and restrain the husband. I tried to explain to Internal Affairs that the husband very badly beat the woman and he was trying to pull my gun from me. As I said before no one pulls a gun on me and gets away with it. I explained to Internal Affairs I did it my way.

So, Ricardo you see I have a reputation for overreacting and I sense that another one of my overreactions may be coming on if you don't quietly leave. He said do you know what I have tucked in the back of my waistband? I said it makes no difference to me what you have but if you reach for anything on your body anywhere I will beat the crap out of you and then call the police. He paused and said asshole you do understand that I have a gun? Then I said did you hear what I said? I have a tendency to overreact and I will beat the shit out of you before you can pull a gun on me. He paused and gave me a smirk. Several seconds passed, he frowned, gave me a dirty look and then he stepped back and turned as if he was returning to his car.

I watched him very carefully like a hawk in prey. I stepped out onto the front porch, dropped my razor and I could see what was about to happen. He turned his body so that I could not see him reach for his gun. I knew better from my police academy and Las Vegas Police Department training that this is a move that requires quick action. As his body turned away I could not see his right arm reach into the back of his slacks but I knew he was going for his gun. I lurched out and pulled him by the back of his neck collar and he fell on his back to the ground. His gun dropped out of his hand and fell onto the ground next to him. I kneeled down and hit him repeatedly in the face with my left fist two times, well maybe three or four times. His nose and cheek were bleeding and I told him to stay down or he would regret it. I picked up his gun and when I stood up I saw a guy open Ricardo's Mercedes front passenger car door with a gun. He aimed his gun at me and I fired one shot with Ricardo's gun that hit him square in the chest. Then another guy opened the rear driver's side door and aimed his gun at me as he shielded himself behind the car door. I fell to the ground and fired two shots. One that hit his right shin and the other hit his right shoulder. I got up off the ground and Ricardo started to rise and I kicked him in the chest and told him to stay still or I would shoot him in the head. I then went over and picked up the two other guns from the two men that I shot. I yelled for my Mom and Dad to come out to the front of the house. I asked my Mom to call 911. I told her to clearly state that two men were shot and one was badly beaten in the front of her house by her son who was a former police officer and that he should not be considered a threat. I told her to make sure that she tells the police that her son is sitting in a rocking chair on the front porch waiting for them to arrive and that he has three guns in a pot on the porch that belonged to the three men that accosted the family.

Now Mrs. Kaster what I am about to explain to you I did not tell the police, my public defender, the court and this was never reported to the news media. I asked my Dad to hide Abdulla in the back of his car in the garage. I told him that after the police left he should immediately get Abdulla out of Las Vegas and check her into a hotel in one of the nearby towns. I felt that if immigration found her and learned that she was in any way involved with the shooting she would surely be returned to China. I didn't want to see her detained in an immigration camp. I was certain based on my earlier research about immigration policy when Abdulla was staying with me in Santa Monica that if she were placed in a detention camp there would be an investigation. Then a hearing that would most likely result in Abdulla being returned to China. I couldn't let this happen. I also felt that it didn't help that Abdulla was living in Las Vegas the United States capitol of gambling and prostitution. So, I thought the best plan was to hide her rather than letting Immigration get involved. Later I found out that this was in fact the best choice given the current government Immigration policy that did not favor Muslims.

When the police and ambulances came there was a basic investigation conducted by the police. I told them that some unknown guy came to my parents' front door ordering my Dad to get Arbella who lived briefly with them. I changed Abdulla's name to Arbella to protect her identity. I explained to the police that when I told the guy that Arbella moved to San Francisco and left no forwarding address he got very angry and pulled a gun on me.

The rest of what I described about me beating him and shooting the other two jerks is what happened. I didn't tell them that Abdulla was from Xinjiang or anything about how I found her in the back of my Amazon van on Halloween in 2017. I didn't tell the police that I was the one who brought her to my parents' home from Santa Monica. For all the police and my attorney knew she was just a lost soul in Las Vegas that stayed with my parents for a few days.

I was incarcerated. There was a preliminary hearing for Ricardo and his two associates Greco and Brown. I was the key witness. While in jail I met FBI Agents Michaels and Daniels and I learned they recently began a surveillance of Ricardo for prostitution and possibly sex trafficking. I asked them if I provided them with incriminating information on Ricardo would they get me a job interview with the FBI. They said maybe, but it depended on the kind of information I provided. What I gave them was incriminating and that is how I got my interview with you.

Now I understand Walt why you had to tell me the entire story. I want to hear the rest but I must leave for a lunch meeting with my boss Tia Lynn. Can you come back around two o'clock so that we can talk about the trial and finish your interview? Mrs. Kaster I can certainly be back at two. I look forward to explaining to you what happened at the preliminary hearing and what has since transpired.

CHAPTER SEVEN

THE PRELIMINARY HEARING

This matter was heard for Preliminary Hearing on January 20, 2018, before the Honorable Chase Guittard, County Court Judge.

Plaintiff: The People of the State of Nevada

Defendants:
Ricardo Sanchez
Albert Greco
Donald Brown

<u>REPORTER'S TRANSCRIPT OF PROCEEDING</u>

Bailiff: All rise, the Honorable Judge Chase Guittard is presiding in the Las Vegas Justice Court, Criminal Division.

The Court: Bailiff please swear in the witnesses.

Bailiff: All rise who might testify and raise your right hand. Do you do solemnly affirm that the evidence you shall give in this matter shall be the truth, the whole truth, and nothing but the truth.

Bailiff: So noted all indicate I do.

The Court: Who is counsel for The People of the State of Nevada?

The People: I am your Honor. My name is Evan James and I am representing The People of the State of Nevada.

The Court: Who is representing the defendants?

Defendants: I am and my name is Lee Kelly representing the defendants.

The Court: First, let the transcript reflect that the original date for the Preliminary Hearing was continued at the request of defendants' attorney Ms. Lee Kelly. I I understand there was no objection on the part of The People. And now Mr. James are you ready to call your first witness?

The People: Yes, I am your Honor.

The Court: Mr. James please proceed.

The People: I would call to the stand Mr. Walter Richards.

The Court: Mr. Richards have you been sworn in?

Answer: Yes, I have your Honor.

Direct Examination by Mr. James

Question: Mr. Richards please state your full name and provide your address.

Answer: My name is Walter Arthur Richards, and I live at 4101 Princeton Street, Santa Monica, California in apartment B.

Question: Mr. Richards let's first get some basics out of the way. By whom are you employed?

Answer: I am employed by Amazon.

Question: What is your job title at Amazon?

Answer: My job title is Delivery Associate, better known as Amazon driver.

Question: How long have you worked for Amazon as an Amazon driver?

Answer: Mr. James I have only been working for Amazon a few months.

Question: Mr. Richards is your employment full time?

Answer: Yes, it is full time but I had to take a short leave of absence?

Question: Mr. Richards why did you need to take a leave of absence?

Answer: Briefly, I was incarcerated on January 5, 2018 after being involved in a shooting in Las Vegas. Once incarcerated I immediately telephoned Amazon and made a formal request for approval of a leave of absence which Amazon generously approved.

Question: What do you mean Mr. Richards by your statement that Amazon generously approved your request for a leave of absence?

Answer: Well, I had only been working at Amazon for a few months when I was jailed after being involved in a shooting. I telephoned my supervisor Ellie

Shawerman from jail and explained to her that I was involved in a self defense shooting and that I was incarcerated. I explained to Ms. Sherman that my absence was beyond my control, the gun involved was not mine and I could not return to work until released from jail. Amazon human resources did a brief investigation and felt that the circumstance of my absence due my incarceration at least for the time being justified an unpaid leave of absence. But the truth of the matter is they didn't need to approve my leave because I had only been working at Amazon for a few months and they could have easily let me go.

Question: Mr. Richards have you returned to work?

Answer: Yes, I returned to work on January 17, 2018 after being incarcerated in jail
for nine days.

Question: Mr. Richards if you were released from jail on January 14, 2018 why didn't you return to work on January 15th.?

Answer: Actually, I got out of jail about midnight and I went directly to my parents' home to make sure that they were okay. I stayed with them on January 15, washed my car and did some chores around the house for my parents. Then on January 16 I drove back to Santa Monica, had an appointment with my long time exceptional doctor Dr. Goldstein and did some shopping for food. I returned to work on January 17th.

Question: One last question about your employment. Did Amazon pay you while you were on leave?

Answer: No and this entire nightmare cost me almost two weeks pay. Plus I had to miss work again today without pay. I never expected Amazon to pay me and I felt very fortunate that Amazon let me keep my job and considered my absence beyond my control.

Question: Mr. Richards you state that you were involved in a shooting. What was the date of the shooting?

Answer: It was on January 5, 2018.

Question: What time did the shooting take place on January 5, 2018?

Answer: It was about eight o'clock in the evening.

Question: Mr. Richard where did the shooting take place?

Answer: It took place at my parents' home on their driveway.

Question: Were both your parents home at the time?

Answer: Yes, before the incident they were both home watching television.

Question: Was anyone else at your parents' home?

Answer: Yes.

Question: Mr. Richards who else was present during the shooting?

Answer: A guy named Ricardo Sanchez and two other guys whose last names are Greco and Brown.

Question: Do you see any of these three men in the courtroom?

Answer: Yes. Ricardo Sanchez, Greco and Brown are in the courtroom.

Question: Would you point them out for us Mr. Richards.

Answer: Yes, the three of them are sitting at the opposing counsel table with Ms. Kelly.

Question: Did you know any of these men prior to the shooting?

Answer: No.

Question: Now Mr. Richards I want you to be precise and please describe the events which led to the shooting at your parents' home on January 5, 2018?

Answer: It was about 8 o'clock in the evening when Mr. Sanchez knocked at my parents' front door. My father answered the door and Mr. Sanchez demanded to see Arbella.

Question: Mr. Richards I am sorry to interrupt you but could you please tell the court who is Arbella?

Answer: I don't know her personally but my parents found her in need of help one afternoon in front of a supermarket. I was told her name was Arbella. Anyway my parents offered to give her a couple of dollars but she refused and she thanked them for being so kind. According to my parents they were about to go inside the supermarket and this woman Arbella started crying uncontrollably. So my parents went back to her and tried to comfort her. Eventually she stopped crying. She told them that she was from San Francisco and that she was looking for a job in Las Vegas. She said that after only being in Las Vegas a couple of days she got an urgent telephone call from a close friend who was very ill. Her friend asked her to come back to San Francisco to help her. From what I understand she told my parents that her car broke down in front of the supermarket and she was distraught because she couldn't get a job nor return to San Francisco. My Dad is a retired mechanic from the RTC and he told the woman that he would take a look at her car and see if he could determine the problem.

Question: Mr. Richards let me interrupt you again. Can you tell the court what is the RTC?

Answer: Oh sure, the RTC is the transit system for the City of Las Vegas and Boulder City. My Dad repaired buses and vans for almost thirty years and my Mom worked there as well in Human Resources.

Question: Thank you Mr. Richards and please continue.

Answer: So, my Dad looked at her car and determined that she needed her transmission repaired. Arbella then had her car towed to a transmission shop to be repaired. Since she had no place to stay my parents offered to let her stay with them until her car was repaired.

Question: Okay Mr. Richards now please continue with what transpired on January 5, 2018.

Answer: Well, I was shaving in the bathroom at my parents' home and I heard the door bell ring. Then I heard some arguing between my father and the person who was at the front door who I later learned was Ricardo Sanchez. I came out of the bathroom to see what was going on and Mr. Sanchez was demanding to see Arbella. My father told him that she was not there and that she returned home to care for an ill friend in San Francisco. Then I could hear Mr. Sanchez yelling at my Dad and he was obviously very angry. I went to the front door to help my Dad. I told Mr. Sanchez to calm down and that he had to leave. He got very angry and crazy. In fact, he was so angry he exhibited all the physical signs of anger. His eyebrows were furrowed, his lips seemed very tense and he had a clenched jaw. I told him it was time for him to leave. He turned and I followed him to the edge of the front porch steps adjacent to the driveway. As he walked toward his Mercedes I saw him pull a gun from his back pocket or waistband. I dropped my razor, stepped off the front porch and I pulled him by the collar of his shirt and he fell to the ground and his gun fell next to him. He started to reach for his gun so I hit him in the face a couple of times I think. I picked up his gun and I saw a guy get out of the Mercedes front passenger door aiming his gun at me and I shot him. I have since learned that his name is Greco. Then another guy got out of the back seat of the Mercedes on the driver side and also aimed a gun at me and I shot him twice, once in the right shin and once in the right shoulder. I have since learned that his name is Brown. Then my Mom called the police. I picked up Greco and Brown's gun and put them in a pot on the front porch. Then my parents and I waited for the police on the front porch. I kept Ricardo's gun in my hand and aimed it at him until the police arrived. As soon as I could see the headlights of the police car I dropped the gun into a pot on the front porch with the other two guns so that I would not be considered a threat. I think three police cars came and two ambulances.

Defendants: Objection. I object your honor. This witness's testimony is too prepared. He is answering questions directly with little or no unnecessary narrative unlike a normal witness would in a preliminary hearing. I believe his testimony is prepared and he is creating this phony story to damage the reputation of the defendants.

The Court: Ms. Kelly your objection is overruled. It does not fall within the scope of the rules of evidence and you may address your objection concerns fully on cross cross examination. If I find that Mr. Richard's testimony was prepared it would certainly concern the court and the outcome of this preliminary hearing.

Defendants: Thank you your honor and you can count on it that I will pursue this fully on cross examination because his entire testimony is a sham and I will prove it.

The People: Your honor, I would like to respond to Ms. Kelly's objection. Her objection clearly implies that I coached the witness and I am offended. If you would let me proceed I can clarify why Mr. Richards's testimony has been so clear and responsive to my questions.

The Court: Mr. James there is no need to be thin skinned and just proceed with your direct examination.

Direct Examination Continues by Mr. James

Question: Mr. Richards have we met before?

Answer: Yes.

Question: How many times have we met Mr. Richards?

Answer: Twice.

Question: And Mr. Richards during any of those meetings did I coach you on how to answer my questions in preparation for this trial?

Answer: No.

Question: Mr. Richards during any of those two meetings did I instruct you on what words to use or give examples of the testimony I wanted you to present?

Answer: No.

Question: Now Mr. Richards how did you know the facial signs of anger that you referred to during your altercation with Mr. Sanchez?

Answer: Mr. James I went to the Police Academy and I also worked for the Las Vegas Police Department for about eight months. At the Police Academy we learned the signs of anger.

Question: Mr. Richards let me now move on to the shooting. I am sure the judge and others would like to know how you were able to shoot the two men without any of them firing a shot at you?

Answer: Mr. James I know why Sanchez didn't fire a shot because I restrained him. As for Greco and Brown I guess I was just faster than them. I went to the Police Academy and I worked for the Las Vegas Police for about eight months. I always did well in firearms training.

Question: While at the Police Academy or while you were employed with the Las Vegas Police Department did you receive any training on how to present yourself in court as a witness?

Answer: Yes, I had course in law enforcement testimony.

Question: Mr. Richards please briefly describe for the court what that training entailed.

Answer: We all participated in a course called Basic Witness Testimony. The emphasis was on being truthful and calm at all times. We were trained how to answer questions directly and succinctly but at the same time always being fair, impartial and objective.

Question: Mr. Richards can you tell me how well you did overall as a rookie while employed with the Las Vegas police department graduating class?

Answer: I was number 2 in my class.

Question: And Mr. Richards how well did you do in firearms training?

Answer: I have a rating of sharpshooter and I was number 1 in my class.

The Court: That's enough Mr. James you made your point now please proceed with your direct examination.

Question: Mr. Richards did the police arrest you after the shooting at your parents' home?

Answer: Yes, Mr. James and I was held in jail without bail for nine days during the police investigation. I knew I was not guilty of any crime so I waived my all my rights including my right to a speedy trial so that the police department could complete their investigation. I even was agreeable to taking a lie detector test, but no test was taken. All the charges were dropped against me and I was released with no restriction on me returning to my home in Santa Monica, California.

Question: Thank you Mr. Richards and I have no further questions.

The Court: Ms. Kelly are you ready to for cross examination?

Defendants: Yes, your Honor we have a few questions.

The Court: Please proceed Ms. Kelly with your cross examination.

Cross Examination by Ms. Kelly

Question: Mr. Richards are you certain that the name of the woman that your parents befriended is Arbella and not Abdulla?

Answer: Yes, I am certain.

Question: Mr. Richards, how can you be so certain?

Answer: Well you are going to think this is strange but I don't think Arbella is a common name. When my parents told me about Arbella I wondered if the Arbella who befriended my parents looked anything like the gorgeous British model Arbella.

Question: You are right Mr. Richard your answer is strange and hard for me to believe. But let me now move on and ask you a question about Mr. Sanchez's gun. Isn't true that you pulled the gun from Mr. Sanchez's back pocket rather than him pulling it on you?

Answer: Of course not and there is nothing in the police report to support that.

Question: How do you know it is not in the police report?

Answer: Because I am not stupid and I requested a copy while in jail.

Question: Are you sure that Abdulla wasn't at your parents home at the time of the shooting?

Answer: You mean Arbella don't you Ms. Kelly?

Question: Okay for the sake of asking you the question; are you sure Arbella wasn't at your parents' home at the time of the shooting?

Answer: She was not present. Only my parents and I were there. As I testified before it was my understanding that she was either on her way to San Francisco or she was already in San Francisco helping a friend who was ill.

The People: Objection. Your Honor Ms. Kelly's question was asked and answered. Further if Arbella was present at the scene of the shooting her name would have been included in the police report. The police report speaks for itself. I don't recall your Honor seeing Arbella's name anywhere in that report.

The Court: Sustained. Ms. Kelly please move on.

Cross Examination Continues by Ms. Kelly

Question: Do you know if the woman who was staying with your parents was legally living here in the United States?

Answer: I don't know anything about her legal status or citizenship.

Question: Mr. Richards you state that you hit Mr. Sanchez in the face two times during the altercation on January 5, 2018. You can see looking at Mr. Sanchez right now that his face is completely bandaged and that he has a broken jaw. Can you explain how hitting Mr. Sanchez in the face just two times could cause that much injury?

Answer: I don't know if he has a broken jaw but maybe I hit him three or four times. He's lucky I didn't shoot him. I don't like it when someone pulls a gun on me.

Question: Mr. Richards you stated that you worked for the Las Vegas Police Department. Isn't it true that you were fired from the Las Vegas Police Department after only working there for eight months?

Answer: Yes?

Question: And what was the reason for your discharge from the Las Vegas Police Department?

Answer: I was fired for using excessive force in a domestic dispute that I was investigating.

Question: Isn't it true that the husband in the dispute had his jaw also broken and was badly beaten up?

Answer: I understand that to be true, but you should have seen his wife who was badly beaten up by him. And he tried to take my gun from me. A police officer is never to lose control of his firearm. As I testified to before I don't like it when someone pulls a gun on me and I needed to restrain the husband.

Defendants: I have no further questions at this time your Honor but it is quite clear that Mr. Walter Richards has a history of aggressive and abusive behavior and that he was the instigator of the shooting on January 5, 2018 and not my clients. My clients, Mr. Richards, Mr. Greco and Mr. Brown are the innocent people here and not Mr. Richard.

The People: Objection your Honor. My client Mr. Richards has not been charged with any crime and is here voluntarily testifying on behalf of the State of Nevada.

The Court: Sustained. Mr. James do you have any other witnesses.

The People: Your Honor we have no other witnesses. Also your Honor the parties have jointly agreed to a stipulation by the parents of Walter Richards. We jointly request that the stipulation be entered into as evidence. The stipulation paraphrases Mr. Richards testimony only as it relates to the time and date of the incident and that they were present. They did not see the shooting because they were inside the house when it occurred.

The Court: If no objection, approved as stipulated. Ms. Kelly do you have any witnesses?

Defendants: I don't think so your honor. But we would like to take a short recess before your ruling if that is okay with you?

The Court: We are in recess for thirty minutes.

CHAPTER 8

PATIME

Mom, thanks for letting me spend the night and I am sorry I slept so late. I never thought they were ever going to finish the paperwork to let me out of jail. I didn't get home until midnight. Anyway, Mom we need to talk. I have no idea where Abdulla is hiding and I am concerned about her. No, Mom I am worried about her. I know Walt but I don't think you need to worry about her now, she is in a really safe place at least for the time being. Where is she Mom? Walt you asked me not to tell you where we moved her to. I know Mom but now I am out of jail and I want to know where she is living. Are you sure Walt? You were very clear with us that you didn't want to know Abdulla's location in case the police department asks you to take a voluntary lie detector test. You said that there would be a good chance they would ask you to take the test since you said you were going to waive all your legal rights and you wanted to ensure that you would pass the test. So, I am not telling you where she is until your Dad gets back from the store. We all agreed it was best that you not know where Abdulla was hiding. I need to involve Dad in this discussion. When he gets back from the store then the three of us can talk about telling you where Abdulla is hiding. You are right Mom that is exactly what we all agreed.

I am going outside to wash my car while we wait for Dad. Oh yeah, later I am going out to Apex Farming. Why are you going to

Apex Farming Walt? Mom, don't worry I am only going to look around. I know what this means Walt and you have something in mind, don't you? Not really Mom, but I need to look around a bit and I will be back home in time for dinner. Then tomorrow I am driving back to Santa Monica because I have to be back at work the next day. The people at Amazon have been very generous in holding my job for me while I was in jail. They really didn't have to hold my job open and I will never forget how good they have been to me as an employee. My supervisor said that everyone was pleased that no charges were filed against me because they like my working at Amazon. They all seemed to know about the shooting and it appears they have been following the story online.

###

Walt, come back in the house your Dad is home. I talked to your dad and we both agree that you should now know where Abdulla is hiding but we don't think you should visit her for a while in case you are being followed. Mom and Dad I don't want to visit her. I just want to know where she is so that I know she is safe. Are you sure Walt that you don't want to see her? Well, I would like to see her but more importantly I want her safe. You know Walt I think Abdulla likes you more than a friend and your Dad thinks you might like her more than a friend too. Mom and Dad just tell me where Abdulla is hiding.

As you know after the shooting your Dad drove her out to Pahrump and got a room for her in a hotel. I went and visited Abdulla in Pahrump a couple of times. I brought her food and visited a little bit and she never complained. She was very appreciative that she was safe. I think she would have stayed in that hotel as long as needed. She asked about you many times. I know she was very worried about you being in jail. Her idea of jail in China was horrific and she did not want you to suffer. I explained to her that the police were treating you well and that you would be getting out of jail soon and going back to work at Amazon. I know this made her feel better but I am sure she still worried about you even though I did my best to lessen her worries.

I hated that budget hotel she was staying in and I wanted to move her someplace else. Your Dad and I talked about it at length and we came up with a plan. I discussed it with Abdulla and she agreed with the plan. What was the plan Mom? We took her to San Bernardino. Do you mean that she is staying with Aunt Harriet? Yes and she is very happy with Aunt Harriet. How did you explain to your sister that Abdulla needed to be hidden? I told her the truth. Actually, I explained the entire story. I told her how you found her in your Amazon van, about Ricardo, the shooting and your incarceration. She was more than happy to have Abdulla stay with her especially because she has been lonely with the passing of Uncle Bill last year. You know Walt she has been very lonely and having Abdulla live with her I think is a blessing in disguise.

Is Abdulla going to look for work in San Bernardino? No Walt, she has a job with Aunt Harriet. What do you mean she has a job with Aunt Harriet? Is she going to be doing house cleaning and cooking for Aunt Harriet? If so I don't like the plan at all and I will move her to Santa Monica and have her live with me until I can find something better. I don't want her cooped up in Aunt Harriet's house doing house cleaning and being a fulltime servant. She needs to get out and go to the store and be productive. Walt, you seem to have stronger feelings for Abdulla than I thought, but you don't have to worry. The best part of the plan is Abdulla is now working for your Aunt Harriet in her accounting office and doing chores around the home. You know Walt your aunts accounting office is attached to her home in the shared duplex. Your aunt and uncle's accounting business has been in San Bernardino for more than twenty years and they are both well recognized in the community as long-time stable residents. No one will question Aunt Harriet having Abdulla living and working for her. By the way Walt, Abdulla is now being introduced to people who come into the accounting office as your Aunt Harriet's niece who is visiting from Turkey. She is working in the accounting office answering the telephone and doing office work. She is fitting in very well and is able to go shopping and out for walks with your Aunt Harriet freely. Abdulla is very happy.

Your Aunt Harriet says that Abdulla asks about you all the time and she thinks that she likes you more than just as a friend. Maybe she even loves you. So, I know she is looking forward to you telephoning her soon.

There is one more important thing you need to know about Abdulla. What's that Mom? Abdulla is no longer Abdulla but rather her name is now Patime. Mom, Patime was Abdulla's sister's name who died in the detention camp. Yes, we know but we all thought Abdulla needed to change her name for the time being until we can get her a green card or visa. Abdulla agreed and when we asked her what name she wanted to use she immediately selected the name of her sister Patime. It was very emotional for her according to your aunt. So, from now on Abdulla is Patime. I think it is a good choice of name. What do you think Dad? It makes no difference to me what we call her I only want her safe. I think the plan that your Mom and Aunt Harriet came up with is very good. Plus Abdulla, I mean Patime is working and learning the accounting business and she seems very happy.

When do you think I can visit Abdulla, I mean Patime? Your Dad and I think you could visit her in a week or so but when you do you can't show her any affection around others. You have to remember that Patime is considered your cousin and people might talk. Talking and gossip is not what we need. So please be careful. Mom and Dad I have no intention of getting emotionally involved with Patime. Walt, that is exactly what your Dad said to me and now we are married twenty-six years. We can see that you both like each other but that you have kept your feelings distant and that in the short run that has been a good thing. However, you both now have a deep connection and things might change. You must realize that you saved Patime when you found her in the back of the Amazon van and then cared for her those few days in Santa Monica. Then you brought her to us and she became a member of our family. These things will never be forgotten by Patime. You actually saved her life. Then you got involved in a shooting and went to jail for her. Not only is she grateful for all that you have done but you are her hero for sure. I don't want to be Patime's hero, I only want her safe. I am not sure how I feel about Patime but I will go visit her next Sunday and then I will know better. I will telephone Aunt Harriet and see if visiting next Sunday works.

###

Hello Aunt Harriet, my car is in the shop and I want to take the train to San Bernardino on Sunday and visit. Do you think you can pick me up or should I Uber it to your house? Walt, I would be happy to pick you up and I can take you back to the train station in the evening as well. That would be terrific Aunt Harriet, thank you. My train arrives on Sunday at the train station in San Bernardino around 9:20 in the morning. It returns to Los Angeles at 8:05 in the evening. That's good, the three of us can eat dinner at my favorite Vietnamese restaurant near the train station and then we can drop you off in time for your train.

Aunt Harriet, how do you like having Patime living with you? I love it and she is a joy to be with. You know Walt she is very smart and a quick learner. In the little time she has been living with me she is already doing some ledger work for me in my accounting office next door. Plus she is getting better at answering the telephone and taking messages at the office. Her English improves every day and you wouldn't know that she has only been in the United States for three months. Of course she has an accent and sometimes there are problems with words but she fits in very well. At night she watches some television sitcoms attempting to learn how people interact in the United States because she says it is much different back home in Xinjiang. I keep telling her that what she is watching on television is more extreme than real life in the United States. I have tried to explain to her that all the criticizing, mocking and making fun of others that she is watching on television is for the purpose of making people laugh. I have explained to her many times that in real life people don't do that so much. I think you are right Aunt Harriet but I have to tell you that I see some sarcasm displayed at work with fellow workers having fun with one another.

You probably already know this Walt but Patime is very excited to see you. I know for a fact she misses you very much. Did you miss her Walt? I guess so, yes I did miss her. Anyway, how do you think Patime is doing in her new environment? She is doing very well. She calls me Auntie Harriet. I love hearing her say Auntie Harriet with her soft accent. It is very comforting. By the way Walt she asks about you all the time and I know she is very excited to see you. Yes, I know you already said that and I think you and Mom are trying to "fix us up". Aunt Harriet, I don't know how I feel about Patime yet. Well, Walt I think she likes you more than as a friend so if you don't feel the same way maybe you should be careful how you interact with her. Aunt Harriet, I like her very much too. But I don't really know how I feel about her because most of my interactions with Patime have been centered on conflict like hiding her in Santa Monica, getting involved in a shooting, and going to jail. Walt, I think you will know better how you feel when you see her today. After I pick you up and bring you to the house I will go to the mall and do some shopping so you two can be alone. That is very kind of you Aunt Harriet but you don't need to do that. I know but I think it is for the best. You know Aunt Harriet you are very much like my Mom and you both want the same thing. I know Walt, the both of us have heard many times during our lifetime that we are like twins.

If you and Patime want to go for a walk while I am gone it will be very safe. Patime fits in very nicely with others but you cannot show any affection towards her in public. You have to remember that she is your cousin and she cannot be your girlfriend in public. I understand Aunt Harriet my mom told me the same thing. At this point I don't know how I feel about Patime. So I don't know yet if I want her to be my girlfriend. But I can tell you this that I am very much looking forward to visiting with her.

###

Hello Walt, did I catch you at a bad time. No Mom, I just got home from work and was about to make dinner. Did you visit your Aunt Harriet and Patime on Sunday? You know I did and you probably already talked to Aunt Harriet and got a full report. You are right Walt, I did talk to her but I want to know from you personally how was your visit with Patime? Mom, it was a very nice visit. Aunt Harriet picked me up at the train station in the morning and took me back to the station in the evening. That is very nice of Aunt Harriet but I want to hear more about your visit with Patime and not your drive to and from the train station. What do you want to know Mom? Do you want to know if we made mad passionate love in front of Aunt Harriet's house? Walt, stop being sarcastic and tell me about your visit with Patime.

Are you there Walt? Yes, sorry for no response Mom, but I am trying to think of how I can explain what happened when we first saw each other yesterday for the first time since the shooting and how we said goodbye to each other. So here it goes. Aunt Harriet dropped me off in front of her house and went shopping at the mall so that the two of us could be alone. I walked up to the front door and Patime immediately opened the door with a big smile on her face and said in very good English hello Walt and please come inside. I am sure she practiced saying hello Walt and please come inside in preparation for my visit. As I walked in the front doorway I said hello Patime you look very beautiful. She obviously dressed up for me and put on make-up. She smiled again, quickly shut the door and then hugged me so hard while at the same time she kept her head firmly against my chest for the longest time. My arms were hanging down by my side and I slowly brought them up and put them around her back and gave her a big hug as well. We didn't kiss or anything like that but I can tell you she was very glad to see me. I guess Mom I was very glad to see her too. This was the first time Patime and I touched other than when she shook my hand back in my apartment in Santa Monica when she thanked me for bringing her clothes from the thrift store.

So then what happens Walt? Well, she pulled me by the hand and had me sit down on Aunt Harriet's sofa. Then she said wait a minute, and I will be right back. With another big smile on her face she came back from the kitchen with the same kind of honey cake she made for me in my apartment the second night she stayed with me in Santa Monica. Only this time she explained how she made the pastry in English. She looked like a beautiful woman rather than a teenager in her red baggy jogging type outfit. She knew I really liked that pastry. I realized then that she planned to make something special for me while I was in San Bernardino, not to repay me, but because she really liked me much more than just as a friend. Then what happens Walt? Mom, nothing much happened but we did talk about my being in jail and what transpired at the Preliminary Hearing. I explained to her that Ricardo said to me at the conclusion of the hearing that we are going to get you. Patime asked me if I was afraid. I said no but that I am being very careful. I also described the guy with the light brown hair and red sideburns that was at the preliminary hearing. I told Patime that if she sees someone like that to tell Aunt Harriet and to then call me right away. Then she asked me what happened to Ricardo and the two men I shot? I asked her if she was worrying about Ricardo thinking that she might have some feelings for him. She said no that she was not worrying about him but that she was curious because at one time he was her friend and he was nice to her. I said Ricardo is okay. I explained that he had a busted nose and a lot of bruises on his face but he will be alright. I explained that he is out on bail and awaiting his trial which is scheduled for June 25, which is only months away.

Patime then asked me what was Ricardo arrested for and I said there were several charges. I didn't go into a lot of detail but I explained that the most serious charge was assault with a firearm. If convicted he will go to prison for maybe two years. If that can't be proven then he will only be convicted for disturbing the peace and he won't go to prison at all. Then she asked me what happened to the two men that I shot. I explained that both of them did not have life-threatening injuries but they both needed to go to rehabilitation. I explained that they are also out on bail like Ricardo and awaiting trial for brandishing a firearm and threatening me. She asked if they will they come after me when they get out of jail? I said no that there was a court restraining order that the three of them are not to come within one hundred yards of me for one year. She said that if this happened in China the people would be in prison now or dead and not out on bail.

I didn't tell Patime that Ricardo doesn't want me to testify against him for several reasons. One, when I testify against him he could be found guilty and go to prison for a couple of years. Two, I think he is very concerned that the evidence that will be presented at the trial may lead to later illegal prostitution or even sex trafficking charges. These kinds of charges are very serious and could result in his going to prison for a very long time. Three, he doesn't know for sure but I think he suspects that he is being investigated for illegal prostitution and possibly sex trafficking. If his employer does not know about all the activities he is involved in it could be very problematic for Ricardo.

Also Mom, I think there is a good chance that Ricardo and his associates may try to persuade me not to testify. What do you mean Walt? I think soon they will try to talk with me and threaten me. Are you hiding something from me Walt? No. Is your life in danger? No, Mom all is under control and if anyone tries to do anything to me I am ready for them. Do you need to involve the police? No, not yet. But I might at some point. Ricardo and his two loser friends have restraining orders and they are not supposed to come near me for one year. Yes, but a gun Walt can be shot from a long distance and hurt or kill you. That's not going to happen so please don't worry. I won't do anything stupid.

Anyway, I think Patime started to get worried that Ricardo may come after me. So, when we were talking I changed the subject and I said that I was going to do everything that I could to get her a green card or visa and she should not worry about Ricardo coming after her. She smiled and said to me, I know you will Walt. We sat there on the sofa and talked for over an hour

She told me about her ongoing nightmares. They were all the same and dealt with the detention camp in Xinjiang and losing her sister. She said she had difficulty sleeping and some nights she would lie in bed awake all night to avoid the pain of the nightmares. Aunt Harriet started giving her a half tablet of Ambien, the sleeping pill that her doctor prescribed for her when she was having problems sleeping after Uncle Bill passed. We talked some more and then Patime suggested we go for a walk.

While walking she said that she had gained a little weight from eating so much fast food with Auntie Harriet. She calls your sister Auntie Harriet. Anyway Aunt Harriet took her shopping and bought her some running shoes and exercise clothes. But Patime said that she felt so embarrassed wearing the exercise clothes because they were skin-tight and sleeveless. These clothes were nothing like the baggy red uniform she wore in camp or like her customary tunic type clothes she wore back in Xinjiang. She told me that Uyghur women typically wear a one-piece dress with a bright vest, baggy sleeves and a head scarf. She said she had never worn anything like her new exercise clothes back in Xinjiang.

Aunt Harriet said that Patime looked terrific in her exercise clothes and that she has a very nice shape. But Patime said at first she was too embarrassed to wear such tight revealing clothes in public that also exposed her shoulders and upper arms. She said that she wore a long sleeve flannel shirt to cover herself up while running in her new clothes. But she always got too hot. So, on the third day of running Patime said she took off the flannel shirt and tied the shirt around her waist to cover up her what she calls her "buttie". She said no one dresses like that back home in Xinjiang. She said at first she felt embarrassed because without wearing the flannel shirt she was exposing her shoulders and upper arms. She said she didn't do that back home. But she said she quickly got over it because it was much more comfortable. She said that during the next couple of days of running her flannel shirt kept coming untied from around her waist. So she no longer wears the flannel shirt while running. She said that she is still a little embarrassed by it when she goes running in the mornings. But she also feels so happy and free while running around the park.

We walked around the park and the area where Patime does her morning runs and Patime said that Aunt Harriet is very nice to her. She said they love to cook together but she misses you and Dad very much. She said that she taught Auntie Harriet how to cook her traditional bread and hand pulled noodles. She also said she loves learning accounting and working with Auntie Harriet and that it is fun and rewarding. I miss her too Walt and I think I am a little jealous of my sister. Maybe I should visit for a few days. That would be very good Mom. I think the three of you would have a good time and Dad can stay home and eat what he wants and watch some sports on television.

I have one last question Walt. How did you say goodbye to Patime? Did you kiss? Did Patime cry? I want to know exactly what happened. Well if you really want to know we kind of kissed. What do you mean kind of kissed? Aunt Harriet was driving me back to the train station while Patime and I were in the back seat sitting quietly and holding hands but nothing more. Patime said to me that she had never been on a train. I said that I would take her on a train someday soon. This is the only thing we talked about during the very short drive to the train station. Aunt Harriet was watching us in her rear view mirror the entire time and it felt a little uncomfortable. We were a few minutes from the train station and I turned to say goodbye to Patime and she kissed me on my cheek. That's it Walt, she only kissed you on the cheek? Yes Mom that is it. You didn't kiss her back? No, I wasn't sure what to do because I didn't want anyone to see us kissing since she is supposedly my cousin and the whole thing felt weird with Aunt Harriet watching us like an owl in the rear view mirror. But I did tell Patime that I was going to miss her and that I would telephone her every night. Do you miss her Walt? Mom you sure are nosey but yes I do miss her and I am going to visit her again soon. Does this mean you like her? Yes Mom, I like her very much. Do you like her more than any of the other girls you have liked? Yes Mom, I like her more than the other girls I have liked. But Mom this is enough with the questions. Do you love her Walt? Mom, I said enough questions. Well Walt, do you love Patime? I don't know yet but I do like being with her. It sounds to me like you love Patime and it is okay with me. I know Mom and I think it is more than okay with you and Aunt Harriet because you both want us to be together.

I have a couple more questions Walt and it is not about you. Did she ask about us? Yes, several times. She asked me how Dad and you were doing after the shooting. I explained to her that you were both fine but that you both missed her very much. She asked if I thought you two would visit her in San Bernardino. I said I was sure that you both would visit soon. She misses you and Dad very much but I think she especially misses you. Walt thank you this makes me very happy and when you see her again tell her that I miss her and love her. I will Mom, I will.

One last question Walt and I want you to be honest with me. Have you seen any sign of anyone suspicious following you? Or have you received any threatening telephone calls? Mom everything is okay. If they wanted to contact me or do something to me they would have done it by now. I am ready for them if they come after me, but I doubt they will. What do you mean by you are ready for them? You know Mom I am not someone that can easily be taken advantage of and I am prepared. Okay but be safe. Goodbye Walt. Goodbye Mom and don't worry, everything will be fine.

CHAPTER 9

THE TRAIN

Hello Aunt Harriet, is Patime available to talk? Of course she is Walt, as she is every evening waiting for your eight o'clock telephone call. Before I have her come to the phone I have something I would like to talk to you about. But first did you know your Mom visited us for a couple of days? Yes, she told me all about it and that she had a terrific time. You know Aunt Harriet my Mom is very jealous of you. She wishes she could have Patime living with her in Las Vegas rather than her living with you in San Bernardino. I know your Mom and I talked about it a lot while she was visiting. I urged her to come visit us as often as she likes. You know Walt it is only a three and one half hour drive from Las Vegas to my house here in San Bernardino. Your Mom could visit Patime anytime she wants. It's not like your Mom and Dad live in Timbuktu. Plus Santa Monica is only a two hour drive for you to San Bernardino. So, we could all get together as a family sometime. That sounds nice Aunt Harriet and I am sure Patime would like that very much. We had such fun the three of us cooking with Patime. One night we made Patime's favorite dish and your Mom plans on making it for your Dad this weekend. Patime calls it pulled noodles with fried vegetables. We also made some pastry dishes that were delicious.

Anyway Walt, I need to talk to you about something very important. What is it Aunt Harriet? Is Patime okay? Yes, Patime is fine and safe here and she is fitting in very nicely. I have been quietly investigating getting Patime a green card. It is more difficult and complicated than I thought it would be given her circumstances of escaping from that awful detention camp in Xingjian. First, I looked into how your marrying Patime would affect her status because she did enter the United States illegally. Wait a minute Aunt Harriet. I don't know if I want to marry Patime and I don't know if she wants to marry me. I understand Walt but I am simply investigating all the possibilities. Since you are a United States citizen if you marry Patime she is entitled to get a green card. However, from what I understand she must leave the United States in order to get one approved. This is because she entered the United States illegally. Also there are many statutes dealing with marriage fraud when an illegal person enters the United States and marries a United States citizen. It is common for there to be investigations that can complicate matters. So, this option may not work but there are also some other options and exceptions.

I have spent many hours investigating getting Patime a green card. Walt I think asylum seems to be her best option. There are basically two paths to claim asylum in the United States. They are referred to as affirmative asylum and defensive asylum seekers. Affirmative asylum seekers are persons who are not in any immigration removal proceedings. They may proactively apply for asylum. Defensive asylum seekers are persons who are already in the removal process proceedings. So Patime would fall into the category of an affirmative asylum seeker. Is that good or bad Aunt Harriet? It is not good or bad it just is very complicated to get a green card either way and it takes some time to accomplish it. If one files all the necessary paperwork a decision can take six months unless there are exceptional circumstances. Also, if Patime filed for affirmative asylum she would probably be detained in a camp or someplace and this could also complicate matters besides being very traumatic for her.

What are the exceptional circumstances Aunt Harriet? I think they are varied and may or may not apply to Patime. But I did learn that there are ways to expedite getting a green card through asylum if you know someone with influence. Do you know someone like that Aunt Harriet? Yes I do. Who is it? I don't want to tell you Walt but she is a senator in another state with lots of influence. We have been friends for over forty years and even though she lives in another state I still do her taxes. Also, she was hospitalized after a tragic car accident when we were in college together. I donated blood for her operation and visited her every day during her three week hospitalization. We are very good friends and we exchange birthday presents each year even though we have not seen each other for many years. Did you contact her? No, not yet but I will soon. Anyway enough talk between us. I will have Patime come to the telephone. Thank you Aunt Harriet and please keep me informed. I will Walt but please do not share any of this with anyone including your Mom and Dad because I don't want to get their hopes up or have discussions about it until we have all the information. I won't say a word Aunt Harriet but please keep me informed. I will call Patime to the phone.

Hello Walt, I am so glad you are calling me and I miss you. When do you think you will be visiting me again? Well, that is what I am calling you about. I have a little surprise for you. Do you remember about a month ago when I visited you said that you had never been on a train. Yes, I do and I would like to go on a train someday. You can and you will. I am taking the train early tomorrow morning from Los Angeles to San Bernardino. Aunt Harriet is going to drive you to the train station in San Bernardino to meet me. Then we will be going to San Diego together on the train. I bought us first class tickets. Walt, is first class expensive? No, they cost a little more than the regular seats. The only difference is that we get reserved seats and a free drink. After we get off the train we are going to then take a shuttle bus or Uber to Sea World. What is an Uber? Patime, Uber is similar to a taxi. Anyway, Sea World is the largest marine rescue center in the world. The park has orca whales, sea lions, dolphins and other marine animals. I already bought the tickets for Sea World and Aunt Harriet said you could go.

I have never seen any of these animals and I would very much like to see a whale. But I don't understand how we can see a whale. The whale would have to be in a very large fish tank and I don't think it would be very happy. You will see what it is like when we get there. Is Auntie Harriet going with us? No, it will be only you and me and you have to remember that we are cousins and we are not girlfriend and boyfriend. We cannot hold hands while on the train. Walt, am I your girlfriend? Yes, I guess you are. You are my boyfriend Walt and I don't have to guess about it like you. Patime, I don't need to guess either; I am your boyfriend. Anyway, Aunt Harriet will be taking you to the train station tomorrow morning at seven. Our train leaves shortly after. We won't get to San Diego until three in the afternoon. Actually, the train goes all the way to Ensenada, Mexico. We have to make sure that we don't miss our stop in San Diego because without a passport or proper identification, you could be detained in Mexico for a long time. But don't worry; I will make sure we get off the train in San Diego. Maybe when you get a passport I will take you there another time.

Once we get to Sea World we will see all the shows and exhibits. Afterwards we will be staying in a nearby hotel. But we will have separate rooms. Then we have to leave early in the morning on Sunday and return to San Bernardino for another long seven hour train trip. I will be ready Walt and I am very much looking forward to seeing you and the whales tomorrow.

###

Patime, I am sorry this is going to be a long train trip. It is only a two hour drive by car to San Diego. But you said that you really wanted to be on a train so it will take us almost seven hours. Walt, I don't mind at all and Auntie Harriet gave us some snacks to eat on the train. I am so excited about my trip with you to Scene World. No, Patime it is not Scene World it is called Sea World. Scene or s c e n e means something you look at and sea spelled s e a is like the ocean. Don't you look at the ocean Walt? Yes, but sea spelled s e a is the water of the ocean that you look at. Do you mean sea spelled s e a is like when I see a bird flying? No Patime, see spelled s e e is a different word than sea spelled s e a. But Walt they sound the same. Yes they sound the same. Then what is the difference between the two words if they sound the same? Patime sea spelled s e a means the ocean and it has water. And see s e e means you are looking at something. So Walt, see spelled s e e and scene spelled s c e n e also mean the same thing. Not exactly Patime. Scene means for example you are looking at a picture. See spelled s e e means you notice something like a picture. Oh forget it Patime and believe me they have different meanings. I don't care what it is called Walt as long as I can scene it or see it with you. That is very funny Patime. You are learning how to joke in English. Walt, what about in your alphabet you have the letter "c" does it mean sea spelled s e a or see spelled s e e? Oh my gosh! How am I going to explain this to you? Patime the letter c is simply a letter of the alphabet and it means nothing else. You know Walt, Mandarin is not an easy language to learn but it does not have so many words that sound the same. What does gosh mean Walt? Patime can I explain what gosh means to you later? Yes, but don't forget because I like the sound of the word gosh.

Uh-oh. Walt what do you mean by uh-oh? Patime, do you remember I told you to watch out for the guy who was at Ricardo's court hearing who had light brown hair and noticeable red sideburns. Yes I do Walt why? He is on the train with us and I am sure he is following us. It would be too much of a coincidence for us to be on the train at the same time. Walt what does coincidence mean? It means when two things happen at the same time like you and me being on the train with the guy with the red sideburns. Don't turn around Patime and look at him. He is two rows behind us. Are you sure it's him? Yes, Patime I am sure it's him and if he is following us he is up to no good. What should we do Walt? You stay here Patime and I will go talk to him. Are you sure you should do that Walt. Yes, I am quite sure. He is sitting by the window and I will sit down next to him in the empty seat and ask him why he is following us. Walt, are you sure this is the right thing to do? Yes, Patime, it is needed and I will do it my way and see what happens. I have heard you say this before and there was a shooting that followed at your parents' home. Yes, I know but everything will be okay.

Hello, may I sit here? I don't care. My name is Walt and what is yours. It is none of your business what my name is. Okay, be unfriendly but let me ask you why are you following us? I'm not following you. I think you are and you are the same guy who was at Ricardo Sanchez's preliminary hearing. I don't know any Sanchez character so stop bothering me. I will but I have one more question. Who do you work for? Look buddy enough of the questions and if you don't leave I will get up and move to another seat. Or it could get worse and I could personally throw you off the train. You are big enough but I don't think so. That's not going to happen but there is no need for you to get angry or move. I am leaving and going back to my seat.

Walt, what did he say? He said he didn't know me or Ricardo but I could tell he was lying. How could you tell he was lying Walt? Because he didn't look at me in the eyes when we talked and I will never forget those sideburns. I know it is the same guy who was in the courtroom during the preliminary hearing. What should we do Walt? Should we get off the train? No, and I know exactly what to do Patime. Do you have any of those Ambien sleeping pills Aunt Harriet gave you? Yes I do, in my purse. Give me three of the pills. Also do you have the kind of lipstick that has a pull-off top or cap? Yes. Patime please give it to me too. What are you going to do Walt? He has a large paper cup with a soft drink in it on his tray next to his cell phone. First, I am going to grind up the three sleeping pills and put them in your lipstick cap. Then I am going to go back to his seat and sit down next to him and as I start to talk with him I will knock his cell phone off the tray onto the floor. When he leans over to pick up his cell phone I will empty the contents of the sleeping pills into his drink. Then I will get up and apologize and leave.

Did you do it Walt? Yes, I did and he was pissed. What do you mean by the word pissed? Patime pissed means upset. Tell me what happened. I sat down next to him and asked him if he worked for Ricardo. He angrily said no and I knocked his cell phone on the floor. As he was bent over I put the ground up pills in his soft drink and then stood up and apologized and left. Three pills should knock him out for sure within twenty or thirty minutes. We are about two hours from San Diego and I will check on him in a little bit to make sure he is asleep. When he is asleep I will take his wallet and find out who he is and maybe who he works for. Without his wallet, he won't have any identification and I am confident that customs in Mexico will detain him. Will he be put in a detention camp Walt? No, he won't be put in a detention camp. But I am sure he will be detained for a couple of days at the border in Tijuana until his citizenship can be sorted out. Why do you think he will be detained at the border and not looking for us? Because, he will be drugged and sleepy from the pills and he won't be able to communicate for several hours. I am sure customs will question why he came across the border in such an intoxicated state without any identification. Meanwhile, we can enjoy ourselves at Sea World and return to San Bernardino tomorrow. Are you sure Walt it will be safe? Yes, I am sure. With that much Ambien in his system he won't be able to communicate for several hours and once he can communicate he won't make much sense. The more I think about it he must have followed me from my apartment in Santa Monica to the train station in Los Angeles. I don't think he has any idea who you are or where you live since you met me at the train station with Aunt Harriet. I think you are very safe. But when he returns to the United States from Mexico he will be looking for me in Santa Monica. But I will be looking for him too and I will be ready for him. What will you do Walt? Please don't worry Patime. I will handle it and he won't be a problem

###

This is your room Patime and I am down the hall in room 305. So if you need me you can pick up the telephone in your room and dial the number 8 and then the numbers 305. I am not going anywhere so if you need to talk to me or if you get scared telephone me. Are you going to kiss me goodnight Walt since you are my boyfriend? Yes, but we have to do it quickly so that no one sees us.

Patime, what's wrong? I am sorry to come to your room but I can't sleep and I got scared. Why didn't you telephone me? I was going to and then I got pissed being all alone. Patime, I don't think you should use the word pissed. Some people might not understand. But Walt you used it when you said the man with the red sideburns was upset. It is hard for me to explain why you shouldn't use the word pissed but believe me it is not the right word for you to use. Okay, I won't say it when I am upset but I think I know when I am pissed or scared. Why were you scared Patime? Because I am not calm being alone. I have always had someone near me at night my entire life. The only time I have been alone is when I was hiding in the warehouse rafters in Xingjian and in the belly of that airplane flying to Los Angeles. I am very sorry Patime and it is okay for you to visit my room. Did anyone see you come to my room? I don't think so Walt. Can I stay here with you? I don't know Patime. Why didn't you take one of your sleeping pills? I couldn't, I gave them all to you. Oh, I see. Do you mean Walt you s e a like the ocean water or you s e e like you are watching something? This time Patime I mean I understand that you gave all the pills to me. If you sleep in my room Patime I will sleep on the floor. I don't want you to sleep on the floor Walt. I am used to it and you are not. I know but it is best that I sleep on the floor. Walt can't we both sleep on the bed? No, I don't think so. I promised Aunt Harriet that there would be no hanky panky. What is hanky panky? Hanky panky means lots of touching and kissing. Walt will we ever have hanky panky? Yes, I think we will sometime. Good and I hope it is soon. I have an idea Patime so that we can both sleep in the bed. You will sleep on one side and I will sleep on the other side but our heads will be at opposite ends of the bed. Also I will put these extra pillows between us on the bed. This way we won't touch. Don't you want to touch me Walt? Yes, I do very much. But this will help us not to have any hanky panky. Okay Walt but I think a little hanky panky would be nice. I know Patime but it is best this way with no hanky panky.

###

Good morning Walt. Did you sleep well Patime? Yes, I think so. I heard you cry a little last night while you were sleeping. I guess you were having a bad dream. I don't remember but I think I cry every night. But Walt last night was the first time I was able to sleep without Aunt Harriet's pills since I moved to San Bernardino. What are you doing with all those things on the table?

I took everything out of the man's wallet and I am examining its contents. His name is Angus Murphy and he is from Newark. Walt is that near the Statue of Liberty? No Patime, The Statue of Liberty is in New York and he is from Newark, New Jersey. They sound similar but believe me they are very different places. Anyway, I now know who he is and why he is following me. Why is he following you Walt? I think he works for the Rizzo Family and they want to know more about how I am connected to Ricardo and his loser friends. He may think I am trying to interfere with their family business. Is the Rizzo Family a well-known large family in Newark? Patime, when I refer to the Rizzo Family as a family I mean that they are involved in organized crime. Walt, I thought because you were familiar with the name of the Rizzo Family they were a well-known family. That is true Patime but not in a good way.

###

It is going to be a long train ride home to San Bernardino but at least we won't have Angus Murphy on the train following us. Walt, are you worried that Mr. Murphy might come after you? No, I am not concerned and if he does I will be prepared. I bought some pastries from the restaurant downstairs for us to eat while on the train. Walt, how long is the train trip? It will be seven hours Patime but we can talk and you can practice your English with me. Actually, I should be practicing my English with you because I think your English is getting much better than mine. Do you really think that Walt? Well, not yet but you are improving so much every day. I like speaking English Walt and I might want to learn some Spanish because there are so many Spanish speaking people in San Bernardino. Patime, there are lots of Spanish speaking people throughout California. Yes, I know and I think I should learn Spanish next.

What language did you speak when you were a child in Xinjiang?

We all spoke Uyghur at home. Is Uyghur similar to Mandarin? No, it is not similar at all. It's something like Turkish. Does this mean Patime that you can speak three languages? Yes I guess it does now that I am speaking English. I never liked speaking Mandarin. There was great pressure on my family and my villagers by the government in Xinjiang to speak Mandarin. They didn't want us to speak Uyghur. The government did lots of things to try to erase our culture. However, we are a strong people and we did everything we could to keep our customs and culture alive. They could force us to speak Mandarin during the day but at night in the privacy of our homes, we always spoke Uyghur our traditional language. I learned a little English in school. English is a compulsory subject in most of China's schools. In fact, many Chinese students begin learning English at an early age. I didn't start to learn English until I was older. In general, they receive their first English lessons in the third grade in primary school. Because we were Uyghur's there was a greater emphasis on us to learn Mandarin and avoiding speaking the traditional Uyghur language. This is the reason my English was so poor when I first arrived in America. But it is not true for most Chinese people.

Patime, what kind of games did you play as a child? We played so many games. My favorite game was similar to your hopscotch here in America. I also liked jumping rope. But we had so much fun making our own clay and clay objects. We always found something to play and we were never bored. We would even flatten a bottle cap, punch a hole in the center, thread it with a piece of string and then spin it. We had so many string games. Some of us would play string hand games and if we got really good at it we could do string hand tricks. We also played many games with sticks and bottle caps like pickup sticks or tossing the bottle cap. We made up many games with sticks and bottle caps. Boys and girls would sometimes play badminton together. But the boys liked playing soccer the most. Girls never played soccer with the boys. Did your sister play with you? Although she was three years younger than me she was always with me and my friends. She was so much more involved with me than her own friends. In fact, my best friend Reyan once said when my sister was sick with the flu and could not play with us it wasn't as much fun without her. My sister was so energetic and full of life and was laughing all the time. She made others laugh because of her own big laugh. I was much quieter and I loved to read and learn.

Did you like school Patime? I loved school and so did my sister. School was much easier for me than my sister so I would help her after school or in the evening. She would rather draw than learn her lessons and she was quite good at drawing for a young girl. I had one favorite teacher when I was in grammar school. She would start the school day with us all singing happy songs. We would sing Raka Rak Dum-Barna and Oyna-Barna which are favorite children's songs. This impressed me and so when I started teaching I did the same thing with my students

What was your home like? First of all our parents were so loving and supportive. They only wanted the best for us and for us to be safe. They were always on the lookout for government people or the police coming to our home. Our home was not big but we did have two bedrooms. The home was made of mud and clay brick that was supported by timber or any wood that we could find. It had a small courtyard as you entered it with a large trellis to the left. We would grow anything we could that was colorful on the trellis but we especially liked growing berries. One of the bedrooms was on the floor which was for my parents. Next to their bedroom was a central room. It had a large rectangular low table where we ate all our meals at. It was a very colorful room. My mother decorated the room with brightly colored wall hangings. Sometimes she would move them around so that the room would look different. This was our common area for our family to eat, talk and read. I loved to read while my sister sat on the floor drawing at the large table. The other bedroom was my sisters and mine which was built just under the roof. It wasn't an attic but rather a room under the roof. Our home was not a two story home but it had an area that was large enough for two cots under the roof. To reach our room we climbed an old wooden ladder that was made from large branches tied together with rope. My sister and I loved sleeping up there because there was a very small roof deck next to our bedroom. At night when it was warm enough we could edge our way out onto the deck and look out at the stars. We would make up games about the stars. Sometimes we would look for animals in the stars and sometimes we would look for large shaped objects.

What kind of work did your parents do? My Dad grew melons and wheat at a local farm. Sometimes my Mom would help my Dad out during the harvest season. My Mom also did sewing to make extra money. My Dad always wanted to be a builder but it was not possible in Xinjiang because Uyghur's in my neighborhood were urged to produce food.

This is enough about me Walt tell me about you. What do you want to know Patime? Tell me about what you were like as a child. Well, I had a lot of friends. We played every sport we could but our favorite sport was baseball. We would all meet out in an open field near my home and play baseball as often as we could after school. Dependent on the number of boys who showed up determined what the rules were to be followed. So, if we had a lot of kids we would follow the normal rules and play using all the bases. If there were only a few of us then we would only play with one base and home plate.

Some of my friends liked to do things that were dangerous or even stupid like damage property. I remember once the four of us were walking in an alley at night on the top of a tall brick wall. It must have been six or eight feet tall and it was not safe because there were no lights and it was not a full moon. It was dangerous for several reasons. One, because there were loose bricks and two, if one of us fell we would fall onto rough asphalt and below. One time my friend Rob picked up one of the loose bricks on top of the wall and threw it at a small travel trailer that was parked in an adjacent yard below. Then another one of my friends Bill did the same thing and broke one of the trailers windows. Then a man came out of the house and started yelling at us. We climbed down from the wall and ran down the alley and escaped. It all happened so fast that I had no idea that Rob and Bill would do such a stupid thing. After this event, I decided not to hang out with them at night but rather I spent more time with my good friend Bob.

I had a lot of fun with my friends growing up and they always seemed to look to me for help when there was a problem. What do you mean Walt? Well, for example, the four of us were at a bus stop in high school. A car pulled up and a big guy got out from the passenger side of the front seat and started to take Dave's coat. Dave was very scared and did not fight back, rather he called for me to help. I told the big guy to stop and he did briefly and then said he was going to take my coat too. I said no you're not. He said yes I am and how are you going to stop me? I said easy and then I kicked him as hard as I could in the balls. Walt, what do you mean when you say you kicked the big guy in the balls? Patime, I kicked him between the legs in his private area. Then what happened Walt? He started screaming and my friends ran away but he still had my coat. So, I yelled at him to give me my coat. Then the driver got out of the car to help the big guy that I kicked. He started yelling at me. He said you little prick give me that coat and then he started swinging at me. So then I kicked him in the balls too. Then the both of them were screaming in pain. I got my coat and I caught up with my friends. Walt what does little prick mean? I am not sure how to explain it to you Patime but it means he was very mad. Oh, something like when you pissed off Angus Murphy on the train. Yes, Patime it is similar but not the same. I will explain it to you another time. You were lucky Walt that you did not get hurt too. I know and there were other times when I did but I don't want to talk about those times.

Did you have a best friend Walt? Yes, Bob was my best friend and like a brother to me. I didn't have any brothers or sisters to play with so I spent a lot of time looking at television, building things and trying to make money so that I could buy building materials and tools. Actually, I did have a sister but she died very young. Walt, what did your sister die of? My sister Mary died of a condition called sudden infant death syndrome. No one could really explain it to my parents but I learned that it is more common in countries that have a lot of money for some reason. I never heard of it in China Walt but I am sorry that you lost your sister. Patime, I didn't even know Mary she was so young. But it was especially very hard on my mother and it took her a couple of years to get over the pain of the loss of Mary.

Walt, you said you liked to build. What kind of things did you build? I liked building clubhouses. When I was about seven years old I built a two story clubhouse made out of wood and cardboard boxes. I built this clubhouse on a vacant property where there was an old wooden fence. Two of the walls of the clubhouse were formed where the corners of a wooden fence came together. The other two walls were made out of cardboard. There was even a window that opened and closed with the flap of a cardboard box. The second floor was made out of several pieces of wooded planks wedged and nailed together. To get to the second floor my friends and I had to climb up on two very old milk crates that we found in an adjacent open field. The roof was made out of more cardboard boxes. I asked my parents if I could sleep in there one night with my friends. They said it was too dangerous and instead said we could pitch a tent and sleep in our backyard. We did this a lot during the summer when it was hot in Vegas.

You said that you liked to make money. How did you make money as a kid? I did so many things to make money. I even sold pollywogs for a nickel when I was very young. I had newspaper routes for many years. I washed my neighbors' cars. My friend Bob and I would go around the neighborhood and offer to install light bulbs in their homes that we bought at the supermarket. Actually, we made a lot more money washing windows in our neighbors' homes. What other kinds of things did you like to do? All my friends and I loved to ride our bicycles and do jumping tricks over boards that were made into a ramp while leaned up against the street curb. Sometimes we would even lean boards up against a picnic bench and make a ramp. My friend Ron broke his right arm on one of those ramps when he fell off his bike. After that we just leaned boards up against curbs to do jumps.

Did you do anything with your parents for fun? Yes, sometimes the three of us would go fishing at Lake Mead. Lake Mead was about an hour away drive from our home and the fishing was always excellent. We would catch the largemouth bass and striped bass. Then we would go to a local park nearby and clean the fish and have a cookout and eat the fish. It was always so delicious and so much fun. Even my Mom liked fishing. On the weekend sometimes Bob and I would get up very early in the morning and take our fishing equipment out to a pond. But we were more interested in smoking cigarettes early in the morning rather than fishing.

In high school I played football and baseball and I was not a good student. I don't mean that I would miss going to school or get bad grades but rather I was more interested in building and doing other things than learning and reading. In fact, I don't think I ever read a book back then. But somehow I got good grades and much better than my friends. After high school I went to college in Las Vegas and I finished in three and one half years. Most kids finished college in four or five years. I got some security jobs that I really liked but I wanted to work most for the Las Vegas Police Department. I went to the police academy and did very well. Then I got a job with the Las Vegas Police Department. I was so happy doing what I wanted to do most. Walt, if you liked working for the police department why did you go to work for Amazon? It is a long story Patime but briefly what happened is that a man was badly beating up his wife and I went to stop him. He tried to take my gun from me. I don't like it when someone takes my gun or pulls a gun on me. Yes, I know Walt, I saw what happened to Ricardo when he pulled his gun out of his pants and wanted to hurt you. Anyway Patime, I beat the husband and the police department thought I was wrong. How could you have been wrong Walt if he beat up his wife and he tried to take your gun? I think the simple answer is Patime that I hurt him too badly. I think if I wouldn't have hurt him so badly I would still have my job with the police department. His jaw was broken and he may lose sight in one of his eyes.

Patime, how about I get us a snack from the café in the next train car? I would like that Walt can I come with you. Sure, and we can use the bathrooms on the way. How much longer Walt until we get to San Bernardino. We have about an hour left. I don't want this to end and I wish you could stay with me in San Bernardino. I know Patime but I will telephone you every night at eight o'clock and I will see you again on my day off in a week. Walt will you let me know if Angus Murphy comes looking for you? Yes I will but don't worry he won't bother me. How do you know he won't bother you? Because I am smarter than him and I will be prepared should he come looking for me.

Patime, we are almost to the train station and I am staying on the train and continuing to Los Angeles. You have to get off the train in San Bernardino and meet Aunt Harriet at the exit. I cannot kiss you goodbye Walt because you are supposed to be my cousin. But I want you to know that I want to kiss you goodbye and I will kiss you the next time I see you. I promise Walt. I promise too Patime.

Thank you again Walt for taking me to Scene World. I am just kidding you Walt. I know we went to Sea World and not Scene World and I want to thank you. It was so interesting and fun even with having the excitement of Angus Murphy on the train with us. I hope he is going to be okay. Patime, he will be okay but he will be pissed. You told me Walt not to use the word pissed but you just did. Yes, Patime, it is the perfect word for the situation. Now I understand Walt what pissed means.

CHAPTER 10

THE LIST

You are right on time Walt again, it is precisely two o'clock. If possible I would like to finish my interview with you before five o'clock. Since it is Friday afternoon I will make my recommendation to my boss Chief Tia Lynn Monday morning on whether we should hire you. You should get a telephone call possibly on the same day from me or someone else in Human Resources on the disposition of your application for employment.

That would be great Mrs. Kaster. I think where we left off yesterday I was telling you that I was incarcerated on February 5, 2018 after being involved in a shooting. Specifically, it was a self defense shooting with Ricardo Sanchez and his two loser friends in front of my parents' home. I am not sure if I explained to you that when I was incarcerated I made it clear to the public defender that I wanted to waive my legal rights to a speedy trial. I did this because I wanted the Police Department to do a thorough investigation of the shooting for two reasons. One, I wanted to ensure that Roberto Sanchez and his accomplices were locked up. Two, I wanted to make sure that when I got released from jail that there would be nothing in my police record that would impair my getting future employment. You already know about my discharge from the Las Vegas police department. I certainly don't need anything else in my record that would jeopardize my securing employment.

While I was in jail Agent Brett Michaels from one of your offices visited me. He said that he and Agent Chad Daniels had been conducting a formal surveillance of Ricardo's activities for the past two days. He said that the FBI very recently got a credible tip from an informant that Ricardo was involved in sex trafficking with minors in Las Vegas. When Agents Michaels and Daniels learned that Ricardo had been shot and I was the one who shot him they of course wanted to interview me in jail. So Agents Michaels and Daniels interviewed me in my cell a few days after the shooting. I explained everything I knew about Ricardo. I lied to both of them and said that I had trailed Ricardo the night prior to the shooting because my parents were concerned and puzzled because they had seen his vehicle outside their house on several occasions. I explained that they live on a quiet dead-end street with a long driveway and they rarely see any cars on the dead-end curve of the street. I said that my Dad wrote down Ricardo's license plate number and then telephoned me. I got Ricardo's address by paying a small fee through the Department of Motor Vehicles. Of course this story was a total fabrication. I felt I could not tell them the truth like I am telling you about Abdulla living with my parents. I was very concerned for her safety and I didn't want anything to happen to her that might result in her being returned to China. I had no idea what they would do with the information if they had it so I kept Abdulla's name out of the conversation.

Agent Daniels said he was also at the same strip club the prior night but had no idea that I was there or that I was following Ricardo. Then Agent Daniels asked me what I knew about APEX Farming. Again, I said nothing about Abdulla or her employment at APEX Farming. Rather, I told him that I had been inside the warehouse some time ago looking for a job. Of course this was also a lie. The information I had about the warehouse I learned from Abdulla. However, I wanted to tell him about the layout of the warehouse in case the FBI wanted to get a warrant and search Ricardo's office. I told him there were two offices downstairs in the warehouse that was used by farming personnel. I was specific and explained that Ricardo had a large office upstairs on a loft in a very private area. I said that I suspected that Ricardo was involved in something illegal. Then I said I didn't have any proof but I thought he was involved in illegal prostitution or possibly sex trafficking. Agent Michaels asked me why I suspected that Ricardo might be involved in sex trafficking. Again, I said nothing about Abdulla. I said because all the women that I had seen him with during my surveillance were young, pretty, most likely illegal and of diverse ethnicity or race. I said that I had no proof at all. I only had a hunch and no proof. He asked why I had such a hunch. I again said that I didn't know for sure but it seemed very strange to me that he drove an expensive car and lived at the Artesian Luxury Apartments while supposedly working at APEX Farming. Then Agent Daniels said to me we have the same hunch but no proof; just a tip from an informant. I said I know where you can get the proof. Agent Michaels asked where? I said get a warrant and search his office. He said there was no way they could get a warrant with the scant documentation they currently had from their only two day surveillance. I asked what if I can get you the proof you need. Agent Michaels asked me how? I said when I get out of here I will do it my way. Then Agent Michaels said what do you mean you will do it your way? I assured them both that I would not do anything that would incriminate the Bureau or make them look bad. Then Agent Daniels questioned me and said you are not talking about breaking into Ricardo's office and violating the law are you? I said of course not but if I get out of here maybe I can get a job in the warehouse while Ricardo is being detained in jail. If so, then I could possibly get some information about him from the people that Ricardo was working with at APEX Farming.

Let me see if I got this right Walt. You offered Agents Michaels and Daniels to go undercover for them. No, not at all Mrs. Kaster; you got it wrong. I only indicated to both of them that if I got out of jail maybe I could get some information that would be of help to them and the FBI. So then what happened Walt? I got out of jail after being incarcerated for nine days. All charges were dropped as I expected and I was allowed to return to Santa Monica and go back to work for Amazon as an Amazon driver. But I did not go back to work right away. I want you to know that both your agents had nothing to do with my release from jail or had any knowledge of what I planned on doing after my release.

Were there conditions set forth in your release prior to getting out of jail Walt? Yes, Mrs. Kaster there was two conditions. One, I had to testify at the preliminary hearing for Ricardo and his two loser friends; which I did. I was more than happy to do this because I wanted the three of them locked up. The second condition was that I had to agree to testify in any other future relevant hearings. Did you agree to the terms of your release? Of course I did, even though I knew the police department did not have a case against me and that my being involved in a shooting was clearly in self defense. But I wanted Ricardo in prison and nowhere near Abdulla, my parents or me.

Then Walt, what happens? Well do you want to know exactly what I did or the result of what I did Mrs. Kaster? You have gone this far with me Walt I think you better tell me exactly what you did. Okay, it was really a lot easier than I thought it would be. But first I had to check to make sure that my parents and Abdulla were safe. So, I went to my parents' house right after getting out of jail to make sure that they were both okay. It appeared to me that they were both fine and life for them was basically the same as it was prior to having Abdulla living with them which I know they really enjoyed. I asked my Dad to tell me exactly what he did after the police and the ambulances left the house the night of the shooting.

He said after they left he went back into the garage and got Abdulla out of the trunk of his car and had her pack up enough clothes for a few days and some of her personal belongings. My Mom packed up the remainder of her clothes and belongings and stored them in the garage on an upper shelf marked "family photos". She did this to hopefully hide Abdulla's belongings in case the police or anyone else searched the garage in the future. Then my Dad drove Abdulla to Pahrump. What is Pahrump Walt? It sounds like a pimple or a boil that needs to be popped or lanced. Very funny Mrs. Kaster but no, it's not a pimple or a boil but rather it is a small gambling town tucked away in the desert about an hour drive from Las Vegas. He checked her into one of the budget hotels and she stayed there for less than a week while I was in jail. While in Pahrump my Mom visited her two times and she did not like where Abdulla was staying. My Mom hated having Abdulla staying in that rundown budget hotel alone in Pahrump. So, she simply decided on her own to move Abdulla to a safer environment. Where did she move Abdulla? I will get to that in a bit Mrs. Kaster but don't you want to know what transpired at the APEX Farming warehouse? Yes, I do so please go on but I do want to get back to where Abdulla is hiding.

I was released from jail on February 14th and I spent the night at my parents' house to make sure they were okay. The next day I washed my car and packed my clothes because I was tentatively planning on returning to Santa Monica and going back to work at Amazon. Late in the afternoon I drove out to APEX Farming. I knew that the warehouse would close around five because Abdulla's work schedule always ended at four-thirty. Abdulla told me that all the farming and packing staff go home at four-thirty. She said that the office personnel also go home at four-thirty and the supervisor and the foreman leave about five.

As the employees were all leaving for the day I went inside the warehouse and I saw a guy who was standing by a filing cabinet in a small office by his office window. I assumed he was the supervisor or the foreman that Abdulla told me about. I approached him and said excuse me but I really need a job. I asked do you have any vacancies. Then I said I really need a job and I will do any kind of work needed including working in the fields. He said the foreman's name was John Turner and that he made all the hiring and firing decisions. He said that he will be right back and for me to go in his office next door and sit in the chair in front of the foreman's desk. Then he said I am going home but John will be right back for sure because he is the one that locks up the warehouse. I did as he said and sat in the chair in front of the foreman's desk. Then I heard the supervisor yell goodbye to me as he was going out the front door and he again said John will be back very soon; so just wait.

After I was certain that the supervisor was gone, I got up from the chair and I exited the foreman's office. I looked around the warehouse and it was quiet. There was no one in sight. I then looked upstairs and I saw the loft and Ricardo's office. It was just as Abdulla described it. There was a long staircase on the side of the building to the loft. It was the only office on the loft. It had large windows with all the blinds closed. Walt, you didn't go upstairs and break into Ricardo's office did you? I did Mrs. Kaster. Did you get caught? Well, yes and no. What do you mean yes and no? I quickly ran upstairs to Ricardo's office to see if his office door was unlocked. It was locked. However, I could see that the door jamb, the door and the door lock were very old because this was an old warehouse. So, I pushed on it with all the weight of the side of my body and bingo it opened. I went inside and shut the door. The office was very tidy and there was nothing on top of Ricardo's desk. The desk had five drawers with two drawers on each side and a middle top drawer. I hoped that the desk would not be locked. I was lucky it was also very old and there were no locks on the desk drawers. First, I opened the top middle drawer and found nothing but stationary, pens and pencils and an old Playboy magazine. Then I hurriedly opened the two right-hand side drawers and found a number of files and some communications but nothing that I thought would be incriminating. I knew I was running out of time and I didn't want to hide or be in Ricardo's office for the night so I quickly rifled through the two left-side drawers and bingo again.

What do you mean bingo again Walt and please be very specific? I found in the left-hand bottom drawer a list that contained the first and last names of at least four dozen women with their ages, height, and weight. Also next to each name was the approximate date the women illegally entered the United States and the country they immigrated from. Importantly next to each name was a rating scale on how attractive each woman was on a range from one to five. Abdulla's name was on the list and she had the highest rating for attractiveness. Also, I found something that was very interesting about this list. As I quickly scanned the pages looking for Abdulla's name I found at least a dozen names that weren't of women but rather they were girls between the ages of thirteen to seventeen. I then found a file that included some communications with what I believed to be with a mob or some kind of syndicate in Newark, New Jersey.

Walt, did you take that file? No. Did you read the file? No, it was too long and I was running out of time so I put it back in the drawer. Do you remember anything that was in that file? No, nothing at all. Are you sure Walt? Yes, I am quite sure because as I said before I was very concerned that I might be caught and I didn't want to hide and have to stay in Ricardo's office all night. Do you remember any of the names in the file? No, I don't remember reading any of the names. Do you remember any of the addresses? Yes, I think there was a letter to or from New Jersey.

Do you remember the address? No. How about any names? No. Did you see any photographs in the file? I don't think there were any photographs in the file. It seems strange to me Walt that you don't remember anything about that file. Mrs. Kaster I felt somewhat stressed at the time and didn't want to get caught. I was concerned that the foreman would find me in Ricardo's office. Mrs. Kaster also you seem to be more interested in the file than the list of names. Is there something about that file I should know about? Walt, I am very interested in the list but I need to do my job questioning you.

Well, I knew my time was limited so I took the list of names, folded it up and slipped it into the inside of the back of my jeans. I then heard some noise downstairs in the warehouse and I quietly exited the door, shut the door and sat down softly on the top step of the staircase on the loft so I wouldn't be heard. It was quiet in the warehouse. The foreman didn't see me sitting on the steps and then I asked are you Mr. Turner? He turned around and looked up at me on the loft and yelled what the hell are you doing up there? I said I was waiting for you by your office to inquire about a job. He yelled again and said who told you to go upstairs. I said no one but the supervisor said that you were the one who made all the decisions about hiring and so I waited by your office. He yelled at me again and said that's not my office and come down here right now which I did. As I was going down the stairs I apologized. I said I thought the foreman would have the biggest office so I waited on the steps upstairs by the office because it looked to be the biggest office. He firmly said to me it wasn't his office and that I shouldn't have gone upstairs. He believed me, calmed down and then asked me what kind of job are you looking for? I got what I needed from Ricardo's office, I no longer wanted him to offer me a job and I knew that APEX farming used a private security service. So, I answered I am looking for a security job. He said they already had a full security service through Platinum Security and that I should contact them to see if there were any openings. I then apologized for taking up his time and going upstairs. He said he was sorry that he yelled at me but he reiterated that no one is supposed to go upstairs. I apologized again and I left at about five o'clock.

You do know that Walt that you broke the law. Yes, I know Mrs. Kaster. However, I sensed that Ricardo was somehow involved in some form of illegal prostitution or maybe even sex trafficking. I thought he might be using the illegal status of young women as leverage to require them to be strippers or prostitutes. The information I found in his office was proof enough as far as I was concerned that Ricardo was involved in the sex trafficking market. Maybe it was not enough proof in a court of law but I was certain he was using the illegal status of young women to coerce them into being strippers and prostitutes. To me this fulfilled the definition of sex trafficking

Walt, what did you do with the list of names? Mrs. Kaster I am very surprised that you don't know that I already gave it to Agent Daniels the day following my breaking into Ricardo's office. You should have received a report certainly by now since a couple of months have passed since I gave it to him. I will have to check the file Walt and get back to you on that.

Oops, excuse me Walt I have to take this telephone call. I am sorry Walt but I have to go to a brief meeting with my boss Tia Lynn who is the one who will determine if we should hire you. Do you mind waiting? I shouldn't be gone for more than five or ten minutes. Of course not and please take your time. My getting a job with the Bureau is very important to me.

###

I am sorry about having to leave you Walt but I am back and I have three questions. One, where is Abdulla hiding? I don't really know Mrs. Kaster. After my Mom picked her up in Pahrump she took her to a nicer hotel in Henderson. The next day she went to visit her and bring her some lunch and Abdulla was gone. There was no note, her clothes and belongings were all gone and no one has heard from her since. Hmm, that seems very strange Walt since Abdulla was so close to your Mom. That's what we thought but I guess these things happen when people are scared and question another's trust. Trust is a powerful motivator Mrs. Kaster. For example, how would you feel if you found out that I was recording my interviews with you? Are you recording me Walt? Of course I am not Mrs. Kaster. I am only using this as an example as to how and why one loses trust just as I would lose your trust if you were recording me. Anyway, I am guessing Abdulla lost our trust and hid elsewhere.

My second question Walt is there anything more you can tell me about the file you found with the New Jersey address? Not the list that you provided with the names of young women but the file that you found in Ricardo's desk drawer. No, I don't remember anything about that file. I was more focused on not getting caught by the foreman.

Now I have one last question. When we first met you said that one of the main reasons you wanted to work for the FBI was that you wanted employment with us because you were concerned about your personal security. Specifically, I think you were looking for some kind of protection. So, now I want you to expand on that statement and explain yourself. Sure, at the conclusion of the preliminary hearing as I was leaving the courtroom Ricardo said we will get you. He didn't say I will get you but rather we will get you. This was a clear message to me that there were others involved in the prostitution and or sex trafficking operation and that my life might be in danger. I know that Ricardo does not want me to testify against him for several reasons. One, when I do testify against him he will certainly lose his case and go to jail and possibly prison for two or three years for assault with a firearm. Two, I think he is very concerned that the evidence that will be presented at the trial may lead to further investigations and it will be determined that he has been involved in illegal prostitution or sex trafficking. These kinds of charges are very serious and could result in his going to prison for a very long time. Three, he doesn't know for sure but I think he suspects that he is already being investigated for illegal prostitution and sex trafficking. And four, Mrs. Kaster I am guessing that if Ricardo works for someone and they are not fully aware of the extent of his activities it could be very problematic for him once they found out he was involved in sex trafficking.

Walt, do you think Ricardo works for the New Jersey address? I have no idea Mrs. Kaster who he works for if anyone. But sitting directly behind Ricardo in court was a big guy in a suit who was not his attorney or someone from the FBI. During my testimony he had his eyes on me like a hawk. I will never forget what this guy looked like because he was big, had light brown hair and reddish sideburns that were very noticeable. I know he was not with the news media because they were all directed by the judge to be in the back of the courtroom.

Interestingly a couple of weeks later while on a weekend train trip from Los Angeles to San Diego I saw the man with the red sideburns on my train. He was sitting two rows behind me wearing the same suit that he wore in court. I was certain it was him because of his noticeable red sideburns. I felt that my life was in jeopardy so I had to do something about it. What did you do Walt? I got out of my seat, went up to the open seat next to him, sat down and then I asked don't I know you? He said I don't think so. I then nicely asked are you from Las Vegas? He said no that he was from Los Angeles. I asked him where he was going and he firmly responded it was none of my business and to stop bothering him. I got up from the seat next to him and I apologized for my bothering him. But I knew it was him and that he was following me to San Diego. Then what happened Walt? Did you report him to train security? No, I handled it my way. What do you mean you handled it your way? Let's just say he was of no harm to me or anyone else for the time being. However, five days later he visited me at my apartment in Santa Monica. He wanted to know how I was involved with Ricardo. Did he threaten you Walt? Well, yes and no. What do you mean yes and no? Actually, we may have threatened each other. Did you find out who he works for? No. Are you sure Walt? Yes, I am sure. Did he say anything about the Rizzo Family in New Jersey? No. Are you sure Walt? Yes, I am sure. Do you think he works for the Rizzo Family? I have no idea who he works for but I do know that I don't want him to visit me again.

Anyway the big guy with the red sideburns left my apartment. A day or so later I saw the two guys that I shot at my parents' home shopping in a supermarket in Santa Monica. They live in Las Vegas and it would be very unusual and coincidental for them to be shopping in Santa Monica. Their names are Greco and Brown and they work for Ricardo. Additionally, there is a restraining order against them not to be within a hundred yards of me for one year. I think they want to kill me so that I won't be able to testify. In fact, I feel certain that they want kill me.

So, if I was employed by the FBI the big guy with the red sideburns, Ricardo, Greco and Brown would not bother me anymore. I want to work in your FBI Human Trafficking Unit. This way I can give my full attention to legally impeding sex trafficking in the United States. I want to help unfortunate women like Abdulla but at the same time have the personal protection as an employee of the FBI. No one is going to go after me if I am employed by the FBI.

Walt, I think we have all the information we need. I will be meeting with an investigation team. We will evaluate all the information you provided and most likely call you on Monday with our decision. Thank you for your time Mrs. Kaster and I do hope you employ me. If you do I promise I will not disappoint you or the Bureau.

CHAPTER 11

ANGUS

That was a really good dinner don't you think Walt? Yes, it was terrific and it was fun watching Mom, Aunt Harriet and Patime cooking together. I think she likes it here with your Aunt Harriet. Yes, she does but she misses living with you and Mom as well. I know but at least we get to visit whenever we want.

How often Walt do you visit Patime? I telephone her every night and see her once a week. How do you feel about Patime? Dad I like her very much but I need to talk to you about something and I don't want you to share it with anyone including Mom. Can you do that for me? I don't know Walt; it depends on what it is about. You know I don't like hiding things from your Mom. I know but the fewer people who know about it the better. Okay you got my attention. Whatever you tell me will be between us. Good and I am sorry Dad but it needs to be this way to protect our family and Patime. I need to sort things out and you are the best one to do this with and you will understand why I need to keep it a secret.

You know Dad that I applied for a job with the FBI. Yes, I know. Have you heard anything? Yes, and it is not good news. Why what happened? I had two and one half days of interviews with them. I explained to them that I found Abdulla in the back of my Amazon van and how she illegally came to the United States in the belly of an airplane. I even told the FBI that she lived with you and Mom briefly in Las Vegas. However, they don't know that she now lives with Aunt Harriet here in San Bernardino or that Abdulla has changed her name to Patime. But it would not be difficult for them to find her if I didn't cover my tracks. They could easily follow me when I drive to visit Patime each week. It is because of this and that I know others are following me that I go to extraordinary efforts to keep Patime's whereabouts secret. Sometimes I call for an Uber to pick me up in the basement of our garage and take me to a car rental. Then I rent a car and visit Patime and Aunt Harriet. No one can see me take the stairway to the garage because I go out my side bathroom window rather than the front door. The window is adjacent to the garage and cannot be seen from the street. I always wear a beard and a baseball cap. Also, I always sit in the front seat of the Uber driver's car so as to look like I am a friend rather than an Uber rider when it leaves the parking structure. If I am being watched from the street they won't know it's me leaving the parking structure and they won't know I am with an Uber driver. Unlike a taxi Uber vehicles only have a small sticker on their front windshield identifying their service. So unless one is close to the vehicle it would be difficult to know the car is an Uber. However, it is very time consuming for me to do this so sometimes I leave my car at work and get a ride with one of the other Amazon drivers and have them drop me off at a car rental. I never visit Patime in my own car and I sometimes take the train. I feel confident that no one knows that Patime lives with Aunt Harriet in San Bernardino other than you and Mom.

Is this what you want me to keep as secret from Mom? Yes and no. What do you mean by yes and no? Well, there have been several occasions when I have had run-ins with some of Ricardo's associates. I don't want you to tell Mom about them or my being followed and the efforts I go to conceal Patime's whereabouts. Plus, I have a lot more to tell you that I want to keep between us only. Okay explain what you mean. At the second job interview with the FBI there was something strange about the questions being asked. Mrs. Kaster from Human Resources kept asking me about a file that I found in Ricardo's desk. I thought you gave that file to the FBI. I gave Agents Daniels and Michaels a list of names that had the first and last names of about fifty young women. It listed their ages, height, weight, country and date that they illegally immigrated to the United States. It also rated their attractiveness. Of course, Abdulla's name was on that list and she had the highest attractiveness rating. If you gave Agents Michaels and Richards the list then what's the issue Walt? It seems to me they already have the list. Yes, they do have the list but there is something else that I found in Ricardo's office desk. I found a file that had copies of letters, notes and photos of young women sent from Ricardo to Lorenzo Rizzo the boss of the Rizzo Family in New Jersey. In addition to taking the list from Ricardo's office, I also took that file with the letters, notes and photos. I did not give the file to Agents Michaels and Daniels. You are the only one who knows that I have this file. The FBI does know however that while I was rifling through Ricardo's desk I saw some letters and notes between Ricardo and someone in New Jersey. They do not know that there were photos of young women and that the communications were between Ricardo and Lorenzo Rizzo.

I told Mrs. Kaster during my interview that I thought I saw some letters that included communications with someone in New Jersey. I lied to her and said repeatedly that I didn't remember any of the names in the file except Ricardo's name. The truth is that the communications were between Ricardo and Lorenzo Rizzo. Why did you lie to her Walt? I had three reasons. First, I thought the file might be of some value to me and I was right. I hope to use this file in my negotiations with Lorenzo Rizzo. Walt, what kind of negotiations? I hope to exchange the file with Lorenzo in return for getting him to get Ricardo out of our lives. Secondly, I wanted to read the file before I gave it to anyone. I did read the file completely. I learned that there were multiple communications with Ricardo and the Rizzo Family concerning business matters. All the communications concerned the strip club business and had nothing to do with prostitution or human trafficking. I wasn't sure that the Rizzo Family was aware of Ricardo's prostitution activities and I needed to get more information before turning the file over to the FBI. I have every intention of giving the file to the FBI if my meeting with Lorenzo fails. I thought when the time was right I would remove all my fingerprints from the file and mail it anonymously to FBI headquarters. This way I could not be charged with obstruction of justice or any other charges because it could not be proven that I was linked to the file. I don't think something is going to happen to me Dad, but if it does I want you to give this file to Agents Michaels or Daniels. They will know what to do with it. However, I don't want you to worry about me because I think Lorenzo will be very interested in the file. What is the third reason Walt? I wanted to do everything possible to protect Patime and the family and I felt the file could be used to our advantage somehow. If my meeting with Lorenzo goes well then our lives can return back to normal. If not then the FBI will be involved. Have you been threatened Walt? Well kind of. What do you mean kind of? I will explain later but just in case something happens to me I need this backup plan. So, will you give the file to Agents Michaels and Daniels if something happens to me? Yes, but I wish I had more information so that I knew you were going to be safe. Dad, I am confident nothing will go wrong. Walt, where is the file? It is inside one of the zipped cushions on my sofa in my apartment with Agents Michaels and Daniels business cards.

There is more that I have to tell you Dad. I learned that the Justice Department is very interested in human trafficking of all types. But they are especially interested in human trafficking of illegal minors. I am certain that when Mrs. Kaster interviewed me she thought that I gained some information about the Rizzo Family when I looked at the file in Ricardo's office. That is why she kept drilling me during my interviews. She kept asking me questions about that file and nothing about the list of young illegal women. I know for a fact that the FBI was conducting a surveillance of Ricardo because Agents Daniels and Michaels told me so. Also, I gave them the list with the names of the illegal young women that I took from Ricardo's desk and they felt the list was very incriminating and that it augmented their investigation. However, the list does not connect Lorenzo to Ricardo's activities. By the way Dad I used a large black marker to cover up Abdulla's name on the list. So they know nothing about her.

I am certain that Ricardo is being investigated by the FBI. However, I had no idea that they were also investigating the Rizzo Family. I am now of the opinion that Ricardo is involved in prostitution and sex trafficking on his own and that the Rizzo Family is unaware of his activities. Walt, how do you know that? Because I had a run-in with a big guy named Angus Murphy who works for Lorenzo Rizzo. Also, I have a copy of another file. This file is an official FBI file that provides a historical overview of Rizzo Family operations in sex trafficking. In that file, it is quite clear that in 2012 the Rizzo Family ceased all prostitution and sex trafficking operations because the then don Frank Rizzo was imprisoned for sex trafficking.

How did you get the Rizzo file Walt? Dad you are not going to like what I am about to tell you. During my last interview with Mrs. Kaster which was scheduled to be only a half-day meeting she received a telephone call. She told me that her boss Tia Lynn requested that my interview be interrupted so that she could join her in a brief meeting. Mrs. Kaster apologized and said she would be back very shortly. She left for her meeting and she did not take with her a file that was on her desk that was with her at my prior two interviews. During those interviews, she looked at the file several times. I sensed that something was screwy about my interview being interrupted and that the FBI was not interested in hiring me. Rather, I thought they were more interested in finding out what I knew about the Rizzo Family and that they were less interested in learning about me. So, after Mrs. Kaster left her office I decided to take the risk and look at the file. I looked around to see if anyone could see me in her office and no one was within eye shot. I got up from my chair and went over to her side of the desk and opened the file. I was surprised by what I found. I pulled out from my coat pocket my cell phone camera and rapidly took photos of the contents. I didn't copy them all but I got enough. Walt you are right, I don't like what you did and it was foolish. If they would have caught you then you could have been shot on the spot or you would be in prison right now. I know Dad but I didn't get caught and I can use that file as leverage with the Rizzo Family to get Ricardo and his associates out of our lives.

Mrs. Kaster returned from her meeting with her boss and began questioning me on what I knew about the Rizzo Family. She repetitively asked me questions about the communications that I saw in Ricardo's desk drawer. She had very little interest in the list of illegal women and the photos that I found in Ricardo's desk that I provided Agents Michaels and Daniel. I told her repeatedly that all I could remember was that there were some communications with someone in New Jersey. I explained that I was very stressed because I didn't want to be caught in Ricardo's office and that I did not remember anything about the other communications. She asked me if the communications were letters or notes. I said that I believed there were both. She asked me why I didn't take the file with the communications. I explained that I already had the list of names and photos which I thought would be proof enough to put Ricardo in prison. She kept asking me more questions. I told her that the file was most likely still in Ricardo's desk drawer and that if the FBI was interested in it they should get a search warrant. Her behavior seemed strange and she said that the FBI will consider my suggestion. It was then that I realized that the reason Mrs. Kaster had to go to a meeting with her boss was because she was listening to my interview and that the meeting was being recorded.

What was in the FBI file Walt? The file is a comprehensive record on the history of the Rizzo Family since its inception during prohibition in 1919. The file includes a complete history on the Rizzo Family, the assassination of Sammy Rizzo in 1960, multiple court case documents, summaries of investigations and lastly a report outlining my involvement in the shooting on January 5, 2018. On the inside jacket of the file is a large sticker that states "Do Not Hire". I then knew for sure that the FBI was not going to hire me but I decided to continue with the meeting as if nothing had happened.

Dad let's get a beer and move outside so the ladies won't suspect that we are talking about something confidential or get their interest. Good idea. I will get the beers and meet you in the backyard.

###

Walt, what did you do with the cell phone photos that you took of the FBI file? I only took photos of the file back to 1960 and I didn't print and of them. I transferred them to a flash drive and then removed them permanently from my cell phone. That flash drive is well hidden. No one will ever find the flash drive unless I give it to them. Walt, do I need to know where the flash drive is hidden? No Dad, you only need to know that the incriminating communications file with the photos that I took from Ricardo's desk is in my sofa cushion in my apartment. If something happens to me then give it to the FBI. Anyway, on the following Monday I got a telephone call from Mrs. Kaster and she told me that the FBI was not going to hire me. Of course, I already knew this since I saw the file with the note that read do not hire. She explained that they were afraid that if they hired me I could be a legal liability. Why is that Walt? There is a concept in employment law called wrongful hiring. The FBI thinks my discharge from the Las Vegas Police Department could be used against them if I got into some type of activity that looked inappropriate, reckless, or negligent like in a controversial altercation or shooting. So, the official decision is that I am a wrongful hiring risk. But the real reason is they were never interested in me and only wanted to find out what I knew about the Rizzo Family.

You said you had a couple of run-ins with Ricardo's associates. What do you mean? The first one was on the train trip when I took Patime to San Diego to visit Sea World. A big guy with red sideburns whose name is Angus Murphy and was at Ricardo's preliminary hearing was following us on the train. I dealt with it on the train my way and he ended up being detained in Tijuana at the border. Since you were a kid you would sometimes say that you would do it your way and it always meant to me that you would get things done. Almost all the time it worked out for you. But I remember one time when you were twelve some older kid beat the crap out of you. So what did you do to get the red sideburns guy detained at the border? I drugged him without his knowledge but more importantly I took his wallet. His name is Angus Murphy and he is from Newark, New Jersey. I assumed then that he was employed by the Rizzo Family. And Dad by the way I got revenge on that kid a couple of weeks later. I will tell you about it another time but he never bothered me again.

I have since learned that Angus Murphy does in fact work for the Rizzo Family. Walt, what do you know about the Rizzo Family? In addition to what I learned after reading the FBI file that I copied from Mrs. Kaster's desk, I did some research online on the Rizzo

Family. I learned that during the great depression the Rizzo Family was quite successful and was heavily involved in gambling, money laundering and numbers. Over the years as the business dwindled due to the legalization of gambling, their focus moved onto prostitution and money laundering. Then six years ago in 2012 Frank Rizzo the grandson of Frankie Rizzo who was considered one of the most successful and powerful "Dons" or mob bosses of the Rizzo Family was convicted of human trafficking and is now serving a twenty year sentence. Specifically, it was proven in court that women were being coerced into prostitution against their will. He gets out in 2032 assuming he is still alive.

As I said before the Rizzo Family has completely discontinued all prostitution operations because they know the FBI is watching them and they don't want anything to do with prostitution and certainly not with sex trafficking. Their focus now is on strip clubs and possibly money laundering. They have strip clubs in several major cities two of which are in Las Vegas that are both very successful. They are no longer considered a major mob enterprise but they are still on the FBI's radar for criminal activity. The FBI is continuing to actively pursue the Rizzo Family because they have been in existence for over one hundred years and they would like nothing more than to completely shut them down.

Walt, you said there have been a couple of occasions when you had run-ins with Ricardo or his associates. Tell me about the other one. Recently, while shopping at the market in Santa Monica I saw Greco and Brown. These are the two guys I shot in front of our house. There is no reason for the two of them to be shopping in Santa Monica. I think they are up to no good. What do you mean Walt? I think they want to stop me from testifying. But Dad I need to tell you more about Angus Murphy. As I said I drugged him and I knew he would be looking for me after he was released from customs in Mexico. It appears my drugging detained him at the border longer than I thought it would. He was detained at the border in customs for four days. About five days later after a long day of interviews with Mrs. Kaster I had my second encounter with Angus Murphy. I opened my front door holding a box of pizza and as I shut the door Angus said firmly "sit down shithead". He had a gun in his hand aimed directly at me. I shut the door and sat down on my sofa across from him. He was sitting at my computer. He said your drugging me was pretty smart but it was the stupidest thing you have ever done. He said that he was detained in customs for four awful days and that I will pay for it. I said I don't think so. He said I have a gun aimed at you and all you have is a pizza in your hand. Then he said, I certainly have a good enough reason to shoot you and yet you sit there on your sofa and say I don't think so. He said you are a smart-ass kid half my age and with half my experience. Then he said what makes you think I won't shoot you? I said because if you wanted to shoot me you would have already done so. But you didn't. This tells me you want something from me. You are right shithead. First, I want my wallet. Also, I want to know what you know about Ricardo and why you beat him up so badly and shot his two associates. Your wallet is in the computer table drawer next to you. I had to borrow twenty bucks from your wallet for an Uber ride the other day but I will repay you. Otherwise, all your money and belongings are inside your wallet. By the way you have a couple of good looking kids.

Before I tell you why I beat up Ricardo where did you get the name Angus? I mean you are as big as a cow but I doubt your parents named you after a cow. You really are a stupid ass kid, you know that? Angus is a popular Scottish name. Ah now I understand where your red sideburns come from. When you were a kid did you get teased about your name? Not much, I was always bigger than the other kids. What about you? Did you get kidded about your name Walt? Yes, I did. Walt, is not a common name and my friends would call me Wally Gator after the cartoon character. I was also called Waltz the dancer. Did that bother you? No, not at all but I have to tell you I would not want to be called Angus. That is enough with the names Wally Gator why did you beat up Ricardo? It is pretty simple, he deserved it. He pulled a gun on me and he deserved getting beaten. No one pulls a gun on me and gets away with it. I did shit head and I got away with it. Maybe, anyway his two loser friends Greco and Brown aimed their guns at me and I shot them with Ricardo's gun. Why did he pull a gun on you? It is a long story but a young woman was staying with my parents for a few days and Ricardo wanted to see her. He was giving my father a hard time so I intervened. We began to argue and then he got badly beaten up and his two associates Greco and Brown got shot. I think the young woman staying at my parents may have been illegal and Ricardo wanted to use her illegal immigration status as leverage for her to be a stripper or possibly a prostitute. Where is the woman now and what is her name? I think she is in San Francisco caring for her friend. Her name is Arbella. But you already know that because you were at the preliminary hearing. So, why are you asking me something you already know? Because, I need to know what your involvement is with Ricardo. I also needed to confirm what you said during the hearing.

Look my pizza is getting cold and I am hungry. Do you want a piece? Yeah, sure but don't do anything tricky. Would I do something like that? Yes, shithead you would. I need to get some plates and napkins in the kitchen. Is that ok with you? Yes, it's okay with me. I already searched your apartment for a gun and you don't have one. You didn't search well enough but don't worry I wouldn't use it. Now why did you have to say that? I am joking with you Angus. Don't worry you have the gun and I am not the stupid one here. You know besides being a shithead you have a smart-ass attitude. Is it Okay with you Angus if I heat up the pizza in the microwave and get some plates and napkins? I promise I won't get any knives. Go ahead but no funny stuff.

Angus here is your hot pizza. Oops, sorry I dropped it on your lap but I at least now I have your gun. You are a real asshole Walt. Here I was being nice and you burnt me with hot pizza and took my gun. Yeah, I am sorry about that but aiming a gun at me is not nice. But now I have the leverage with the gun and you don't. So now I have some questions. Do you work for the Rizzo Family? What makes you think I work for the Rizzo Family? Because when I rifled through Ricardo's desk drawer I found something. What did you find? You know both you and the FBI seem to be interested in that file. What do you mean the FBI is interested in the file? Well Angus, I am applying for a job with the FBI. But I don't think they are going to hire me. In fact, I just finished a long day of interviews with them. What did you tell them? I told them that I believed Ricardo was involved in prostitution and possibly human trafficking which included minors. What did you tell the FBI about the Rizzo Family? I told them that I knew nothing about the Rizzo Family. But between you and me I think that the Rizzo Family has nothing to do at all with prostitution or human trafficking. I think that they are only involved in strip clubs and possibly money laundering. I think the reason you are following me is to find out how I am involved with Ricardo and whether or not your boss wants to get rid of me.

My next question is can you get me a meeting with Lorenzo Rizzo the great-grandson of Frankie Rizzo? How do you know he is the great-grandson of Frankie Rizzo? Let me answer it this way. I have done some research and I have some very pertinent information that would be of significant value to him. What do you want in return? I want Ricardo and his two loser associates Greco and Brown out of my life. I think they are planning on killing me because Ricardo does not want me to testify at his June

25 hearing. I saw the two of them at a market here in Santa Monica and they live in Vegas. It makes no sense for the two of them being here other than they are after me. You know kid if I set up this meeting with Lorenzo and you don't deliver it will not only be your ass but mine. Angus don't you think we have come a long way and should now be able to trust one another? You drugged me, took my wallet, spilled hot pizza on me and then took my gun and you think I should trust you. Yes, I do and I think you understand that I can be very helpful to Lorenzo. By the way, I told you earlier Angus that no one pulls a gun on me and gets away with it. But I am going to give you your gun back and get us a beer from the refrigerator to have with our pizza. You are not going to shoot me and I am not going to shoot you. So why don't you call me Walt rather than shithead or kid while we dine together? By the way, Angus I do have a gun taped to the underside of the sink in the kitchen but I would never use it on you.

###

You are lucky Walt that Angus believed you and didn't shoot you in your apartment. Dad I never felt threatened by Angus even though he had a gun pointed I knew all he wanted from me was information and I gave it to him. Walt, when are you meeting with Lorenzo Rizzo? I am meeting with him in a couple of days.

CHAPTER 12

THE RIZZO FAMILY FBI FILE

FEDERAL BUREAU OF INVESTIGATION

TO: Red Bank, New Jersey Office

Date:March 2, 2018

From: Las Vegas Office

Drafted by: Agent B. Michaels
Agent C. Daniels

Approved by: Chief T. Lynn

Case ID #: 1562.1810.1736

Subject: Historical Overview of Rizzo Family Operations in Sex Trafficking

Executive Summary:

For many decades the Rizzo Family business has been heavily involved in prostitution and sex trafficking. The Family has experienced two major business setbacks. The first was in 1960 with the assassination of the then boss Sammy Rizzo and his underboss Giacamo Vitelli. The second was with the conviction and imprisonment in 2012 of the former boss Frank Rizzo. It is believed that Lorenzo Rizzo, the succeeding boss, ceased all forms of prostitution including sex trafficking in 2012.

The Rizzo Family has successful strip clubs in major cities. We suspect that these clubs are used for money laundering but we have no corroboration. Recently, we learned through an informant that the Rizzo Family may again be involved in prostitution and sex trafficking in Las Vegas, Nevada. This has not been confirmed. We received a credible tip from a reliable informant that the Rizzo Family is in fact involved in illegal prostitution and sex trafficking in Las Vegas that includes minors. Agent B. Michaels and C. Daniels are now in Las Vegas and have an ongoing surveillance underway of Ricardo Sanchez. He works for the Rizzo Family and is the prime target of our investigation. Our informant states that she is certain that Ricardo Sanchez is leading the operation in Las Vegas.

Ricardo Sanchez is out on bail awaiting a hearing on criminal charges not related to prostitution, sex trafficking or money laundering. Agents Michaels and Daniels report that they have interviewed a Walter Richards who is employed as an Amazon driver. He was incarcerated at the same time as Ricardo Sanchez following a shooting at his parents' home on January 5, 2018. Ricardo Sanchez and his two associates Albert Greco and Donald Brown harassed Walter Richards at the Richards' family's home on January 5, 2018 and threatened him with firearms. Somehow Walter Richards severely beat up Sanchez and shot Greco and Brown with Sanchez's gun. No charges have been filed against

Walter Richards. Sanchez, Greco and Brown are out on bail awaiting trial set for June 25, 2018.

On January 16, 2018 Walter Richards provided Agents Michaels and Daniels with a list that contains names of young women. He independently secured this list through illegal means. It is believed that all of these young women are illegally in the United States and many are employed as strippers or prostitutes reporting to Sanchez. Our informant reported to us that Ricardo Sanchez is using the illegal status of these young women to coerce them to be strippers and prostitutes in Las Vegas. If we can prove this then we can move to indict Lorenzo Rizzo which will then finally abolish Rizzo Family operations.

It should be noted that Walter Richards, an Amazon driver, secured an employment interview with the Bureau in exchange for providing the FBI with above list. He has an upcoming interview on March 14, 2018 with FBI Human Resources Manager R. Kaster. The bureau has no interest in employing Walter Richards. We think Walter Richards is a danger. He is unpredictable and if hired might cause unintentional legal liability and harm to the Bureau.

Introduction:

The following is not pertinent to our current investigation of the Rizzo Family in Las Vegas. We are providing the information to give insight into the:

- Internal workings of the Rizzo Family up until only 1960. However, we believe the basic policies of the organization are still in place today.
- Conflicts within the Rizzo Family business and a historical overview of its operations.
- The Rizzo Family five rules which we believe are still in

effect today. These rules need to be highlighted in this report so that we have a better understanding of what happens if a Family member violates the rules.

- Events that led up to the assassination of Sammy Rizzo and his underboss Giacamo Vitelli in 1960.
- Specifics of Sammy Rizzo and Giacamo Vitelli's 1960 assassinations. Although, both their assassinations are not related in any way to our current investigation in Las Vegas we are concerned that Walter Richards may try to assassinate Lorenzo Rizzo. We suspect this because Walter Richards:
    1. Has already severely beaten Ricardo Sanchez and shot both Albert Greco and Donald Brown. All three of these individuals are connected to the Rizzo Family.
    2. Motivation is unknown as to how or why he illegally obtained the list that he provided to Agent Michaels and Daniels.
    3. True motivation may be revenge against Lorenzo Rizzo or Family members. However, we have no evidence that supports this assertion.

Background:

The Rizzo Family has been operating as an organized syndicate since the passage of the 18th Amendment in 1919 which prohibited the manufacture, sale, or transportation of intoxicating liquors. They were considered a smaller operation focusing on speakeasies in suburbs rather than in major cities. As business declined with the repeal of the 18th Amendment in 1934 they shifted their efforts to numbers and prostitution. The Family grew in influence and power with gambling and prostitution as their major source of income. Sammy Rizzo was assassinated in 1960. Although Cuba was not the initiator of the "hit", funds were transferred through Castro's regime. From 1960 through present various Rizzo children have inherited control of Rizzo Family operations.

Sammy Rizzo and his underboss Giacamo Vitelli were both assassinated on June 16, 1960. They were assassinated at the hands of the Family accountant Clarence Wilson who had worked for the Family for many years. The reasons for these assassinations are complex. However, it was well publicized in a letter prepared by the assassin Clarence Wilson that was sent to the Bureau and major news outlets. Following are copies of two letters sent in 1960. The first letter was sent to major newspapers and the FBI explaining the inner working of the Rizzo Family in 1960. The second letter was sent to Sammy Rizzo and his underboss Giacamo Vitelli giving them notice that they would be assassinated.

Clarence Wilson Letters:

Letter #1 May 1, 1960

I am sending this to The New York Times, The Washington Post, USA Today, Chicago Tribune, The Boston Globe, The Wall Street Journal, The Los Angeles Times and you. You are getting this because I am dead and possibly one of my Family members has had a bizarre or unexplained accident. I want you to read this very carefully before you do anything with it. You may publish it and or send it to the cops or the Feds. I don't care because once you read it you will do something with it that will please me.

My name is Clarence Wilson and I am the accountant for the Rizzo Family. I have worked for the Family for twenty-nine years. I know you know who the Rizzo Family is and the key players. But you do not know the inner workings of the Family or how individuals interact with Sammy Rizzo. If you think you do know I am telling you that you don't. Most of the Rizzo soldiers don't know for sure because Sammy Rizzo is very controlling. I know that the Feds have a pretty good idea but they are not certain either.

I am going to tell you so that there is no question who's who and what their positions and responsibilities are within the Rizzo Family. I am going to explain it to you as if you know very little. Sammy Rizzo of course is the boss or don and is known as Sammy "The Genius". The reason he is called the genius is he went to Harvard for a short time. However, he had to quit school to help his brother Frankie Rizzo run the Family after he was diagnosed with cancer. Once diagnosed with cancer he lasted only about a month and Sammy had to step in and replace Frankie. That was the end of Sammy's time at Harvard.

Sammy's underboss is Giacamo Vitelli and he is second in command. He is a mean son of a bitch who acts quickly and sometimes does not think. Everyone below him is afraid of him because of his impulsive and sometimes erratic behavior. But Sammy likes him very much because he is loyal and would give his life for him. Giacamo runs most of the day to day operations with the exception of security. This is not to say that he doesn't ever get involved with security issues because he does but only when Sammy says it's ok. The reason is that Sammy is concerned that Giacamo might do something that is an overreaction so this way he keeps him under control.

The consigliore or the counselor is Anthony Capello. He is third in command and attends almost all of Sammy's meetings. If he is not at the meeting it is because Sammy wants him somewhere else. He gives advice on all matters but only when asked by Sammy. Otherwise he is quiet during meetings. Sammy does not like others to advise him. Sammy uses Taylor and Taylor. They are an outside law firm that handles all litigation and court matters. Even though Anthony is not an attorney he is well versed on the law. He is in his late 70's and has been with the Family for over fifty years so he has a lot of experience.

There are four Captains or Capo's that report directly to Sammy but also take orders from Giacamo the underboss. Frank Sattella is over drugs, Paulie Rosetti is over prostitution, Paulie Ricca is over gambling, money laundering and numbers and Albert Molino is over Security which I will tell you about later. The two Paulie's have nick names. Paulie Rosetti goes by the nickname "The Joker" because he's always ready with a quick joke. Paulie Ricca goes by the nickname "Squinty" because whenever he is in the sun or under bright lights he has a very noticeable squint. As I said Albert Molino is over security. He takes orders only from Sammy. His job title should actually be the enforcer. He handles all strong arming and hits or what your newspapers like to call whacks. You will recall a couple of years ago Gilbert Thompson the president of SBS TV was shot two times in the head for unknown reasons while watering his roses in the front yard. That was personally done by Molino. It is rare for him to do a hit since he is a captain but he did the job rather than one of his soldiers. The reason that Thomson was hit by Molino was he was planning a three part TV series on mobs with a major focus on Sammy. I was in the room when the hit was ordered by Sammy. Sammy told Molino to personally do the hit.

I started keeping a record of hits and payoffs about ten years ago. Although I am aware of many more jobs the attached list only goes back to 1950 since I did not keep records until then. You will note there are three columns listing payoffs, strong-arming politicians and persons of influence and hits. I have included dates and notes of what I know. The Feds will be very interested in this document.

All the captains are made men. Reporting to the captains are the soldiers. Some bright but most are a bunch of losers who will do whatever they are asked for money, recognition and status of being attached to the Rizzo Family. They do all the day to day jobs and dirty work.

Lastly, there is me. I started working for the Rizzo Family in 1931 right in the middle of the depression. I met Frankie Rizzo in a small diner on the east side. I was in the diner studying and he walked by my table, leaned over to me and asked me what I was reading. I told him I was studying for my last accounting exam at the community college. He asked me if I got good grades and I told him that I got all A's. He then asked me how did I support myself and go to school. I told him I did custodial work at night and sometimes I did odd jobs. He then asked me what kind of odd jobs and I told him I would rather not tell him. He then smiled and said I know times are tough and that when I graduated from community college if I wanted a job to call Tony Costello and he would give me a job. I did and I have been working for the Rizzo Family for 29 years. Tony was a nice guy and taught me a lot during the nine years I worked for him. He died about twenty years ago of natural causes and I moved up to be the accountant reporting directly to the consigliore. I have attached an organization chart that identifies all the current members of the Family.

When working for the Rizzo Family it is important to know that there are five rules that can never be violated without repercussions.

RULE 1: Nothing is ever in writing to Sammy or Giacamo. Anytime there is a need to communicate with Sammy or Giacamo it must be in person or on a private phone line and never on a public phone. There are no exceptions. If you have a message for Sammy you whisper it in his left ear-never in his right ear. Only in his left ear because Sammy has a hearing problem and refuses to wear a hearing aid. So as to not to bring any attention to Sammy's poor hearing Giacamo also receives messages only in his left ear. It makes no difference who violates the rule. If it is a minor infraction like giving a phone number on a piece of paper without approval then one can be fined up to $1,000. If it's a very serious violation like reporting on the status of an illegal activity the outcome could be severe like getting popped or going missing. Everyone knows that Sammy is always concerned that someone is listening and he is very protective of communications. For some reason he does not have any problem with getting messages on his private phone line even though he knows the Feds have ways of tapping phones.

RULE 2: Never finger anyone. This is one of the most serious offenses. If someone is caught informing they get popped and so does one of their personal family members. If you get arrested, do time and don't rat then your family is taken care of until you're out. Everyone is expected to support the Family and never say anything negative about the Family to anyone.

RULE 3: No fighting among Family members. Anyone caught fighting will get fined at least $1,000. I remember when two soldiers got in a fight over a girl and one was hospitalized. Both got fine $2,000. Of course verbal arguments are ok and common place.

RULE 4: No skimming. Anyone caught skimming or doing business on the side gets seriously injured or goes missing dependent how egregious they violated the rule. About a year ago Bobbie Protudo had his ear clipped for pocketing $50.

RULE 5: There is an unspoken rule. No one ever leaves or retires from the Family. If you ask to leave or give any hint that you're thinking of leaving you will go missing. Not popped but go missing. It is the same thing but no one knows for sure what happened. If you actually leave the Family one of your own family members will have a serious accident that will most likely end in death. There are very few exceptions to this policy. Tubby Jensen a soldier had a major heart attack and then a stroke while in the hospital. Ultimately he went into a coma and was a vegetable for many months. The Rizzo Family paid all his medical bills and gave his wife some money after he died. Some referred to it as his retirement pension. This is not to say that there isn't talk especially among soldiers about alternatives to leaving or retiring. There is common joking and casual dialogue about retiring in Sicily in hopes that Sammy would pick up on the idea and someday approve of Family members retiring in Sicily. The captains were especially fond of this idea and would freely joke about it among themselves and with the soldiers.

This brings me to why I am writing you. I wanted out and I know that there is no way Sammy would approve my leaving even though he trusts me. What I have done violates all five rules. I knew that when I started keeping records that I had to be very careful and that I would have to develop a plan that would be fool proof to get out and protect my family. I knew that even if I left the country with my wife, my kids and my grandkids, any relatives still here in the U.S. would be at risk. I could not let this happen. I knew ten years ago that I would need a lot of money to implement a plan that would protect my entire family. What I did was very risky. However, I didn't get caught back then and if you are reading this now you know that I have since been caught.

As you probably know the Rizzo Family never saves money. They only invest in property and never in banking. In 1950 I started skimming money that went into separate expense accounts for such things as utilities for warehouses that didn't have utility bills. There were mortgages that were for properties that did not exist. I refinanced a few properties and deposited the money into accounts that were supposed to be used for paying taxes but the money was always held and never paid. I had accrued over $500,000. On May 1, 1960 all the money was wired to an account in Cuba. In 1959 Castro overthrew the government and became Prime Minister. I developed some connections in Cuba because the

Rizzo Family had casino investments in Havana. I built a relationship with one of Castro's key staff that I will call Mr. X. I assisted him in shifting a very large sum of money from Batista's holdings to Castro. My actions helped to solidify Castro's takeover of the Batista regime. After the transaction was completed Mr. X telephoned me. He said that Castro personally told him that if I ever needed anything done in Cuba to contact Mr. X. There would be no questions and it would be done. I have since contacted Mr. X requesting his assistance. I wired Mr. X $100,000 with specific instructions. All of the money would be for one purpose. $75,000 was for a hit on the boss Sammy Rizzo and $25,000 for the underboss Giacamo Vitelli. The hits are to be done by former U.S. Feds who both have prior military sniper experience. I will say this about both of these men. They both have lots of connections and have done several successful hits each. Both have no allegiance to anyone and there is no one currently in the Ike administration that would bother them. Each man only knows about his assigned hit and does not know that there are two hits being done in the Rizzo Family. Mr. X was substantially paid in advance for his services and I trust him and Castro.

Mr. X was to wire the money to the two men if something happened to me. Both men knew that the job had to be done quickly and they were anxious and gladly wanting to do the hits for a variety of reasons. One reason of course was for the money but another was revenge. Both men hated the Rizzo Family for reasons I won't go into again to protect their identity.

The hits had to be done immediately to protect my own family members. By eliminating Sammy and Giacamo at the same time would put the Family into mass confusion and out of control. Additionally, this document going to the Feds and the press would expose the Family and would spiral into chaos. Captains and soldiers would have no alternative but to run and hide.

So, I am guessing at this point you are wondering how I would leave the Family and protect myself and my family and at the same time not have to do the two hits. This is where the following undated letter comes in that were sent to both Sammy Rizzo and Giacamo Vitelli. If you are reading it now I am dead. I want you to know that I did everything possible to protect my Family.

Letter #2 Undated

Sammy and Giacamo

I have left the Family. My twenty-nine years with the Family is enough and I am retiring. I did good work for you but at the same time I have protected myself. I know what you are thinking that no one retires. But I am. If you come after me you both will be hit. I have skimmed more than enough money to clip you both and it will happen if you come after me or any of my Family members. By the way you will both be hit at about the same time. You know that if this happens the Family will go into chaos. None of your captains can pick up the pieces and run the organization. You both understand that the consigliore Anthony is too old. This means that your personal loved ones will be left without any protection or financial support. If I am hit or injured by you a package is being sent to all the major news media and the Feds. The package includes this letter, documents outlining Family activities and hits over the past ten years. Actually, I am quite impressed with what I prepared. I think it would make a good book. Anyway you have two alternatives. The first is you leave me and my family alone. By the way I have left the country. Try to find me and hurt any of my personal family members then the package will be mailed immediately. The second alternative is for you to do nothing. You can make whatever excuses you want to the captains about my whereabouts. Or you can let them think I have gone missing as has happened to others who have violated Rizzo Family rules. You know they all will go along with whatever you say and the topic will be finished. The choice is yours.

In the future you might consider the possibility of Family members retiring in Sicily.

Regards,

Clarence Wilson, Accountant   May 1, 1960

CHAPTER 13

LORENZO

It's me Aunt Harriet and I am sorry I did not telephone Patime last night. Was she upset? No she was not upset but she was worried about you. I know. I am glad she is learning how to text because I received a couple of her messages last night stating that she was worried about me. I responded to her saying that I had to work a double shift. But I didn't. What do you mean you didn't have to work? I can't go into the details with you but I think I am getting close to getting Ricardo and his associates out of our lives. That is great news Walt. Have the police secured more incriminating information on them that would result in their being locked up for a long time. Yes and no. What do you mean by yes and no? Well I am working with the FBI and others but I don't want to go into the details with you. Walt, I hope the police or the FBI find something more incriminating because it is my understanding that if they are found guilty of the current charges then they won't be locked up long enough for Patime and you to be safe. We are all concerned that when they get out of jail or prison they will come after you and possibly Patime. I know Aunt Harriet but it is going to work out, so not to worry. I hope so Walt, I hope so.

Anyway may I speak to Patime? She just left to go running but she will be back in about forty-five minutes. Okay please tell her that I will call her tonight from the airport. Walt, why are you going to the airport? Again, I don't want to go into the details but I am working on something that will hopefully resolve our Ricardo problem. Walt, I hope you are doing something that is safe and legal. I think it is safe and legal Aunt Harriet. I have found over the years Walt what you think is safe and what others think is safe isn't necessarily safe. I understand Aunt Harriet but please don't worry and by all means, don't tell my mom. Now you really have me concerned. If you don't want your mom to know you are going to the airport then there is something for me to worry about. Aunt Harriet, like my mom you are a bit of a "worry wart" and I don't want to worry either of you.

Do you have any news from your senator friend about getting Patime a Green Card? Yes and no. Aunt Harriet, now you sound like me by saying yes and no. What do you mean by yes and no? My senator friend said that there is no current procedure or law that would allow her to get a Green Card for Patime. She said that even the President of the United States does not have that authority. But she said it is not impossible to get her a Green Card. Interestingly I learned that there may be a United States policy that limits how many people of a particular race can be approved for a Green Card each year. Since the United States can't really limit immigration by race, it is done by country. Because Patime is from China she may be better off securing a Green Card than let's say someone from El Salvador. But maybe not. The number of Uyghurs coming to the United States is minuscule compared to other immigrants.

There is however another mechanism to get a Green Card. My senator friend said that it is possible for a senator to introduce a "private bill" to legislatively confer permanent residence rights or even citizenship for someone who is illegally in the United States. I explained in detail to my senator friend the horrific conditions that Patime and other Uyghurs endured in Xinjiang China. She said that she would support submitting a bill that would make Patime's residence in the United States legal. She said if she could accomplish this then Patime's legal status would be resolved and no one like Ricardo could threaten her with turning her into Immigration. Additionally, she said that senators can intercede and use their oversight authority to expedite the Green Card process. The process is very bureaucratic but getting a Green Card for Patime may in fact be possible.

Aunt Harriet, this sounds very positive to me. Yes, it is Walt but there is a big stumbling block. What is the stumbling block? My senator friend needs the support of the senate and she may not have the votes. When will your senator friend introduce the bill? She said she needs to meet with other senators but hopefully she will know if she can get the votes and introduce the bill in the next couple of weeks. The good news is that the current administration recognizes China's atrocities against the Uyghurs as genocide. However, the United States is still doing business in Xinjiang. She said if Patime would testify before the Subcommittee on Human Trafficking it would help her get the votes. Patime has reluctantly agreed. She said that she felt that if she had to testify and had to explain what happened to her in the detention camp and in the black room it would be very emotional and embarrassing. But she said she would do it if necessary to stay in the United States. Also, she misses her parents very much. Once she has a green card she will be able to send mail to them. Currently, she can't write to them because the United States Immigration Service might track her living here in San Bernardino. She has tried telephoning them using the free Skype at the library but there have been no answers. I explained to Patime that she needs to be very careful attempting to telephone her parents and that she cannot use any landlines or cell phones because someone might be able to trace her location. She is very worried about them. She said she has no idea if they are alive or if they have left Xinjiang. And they have no idea if she is dead or alive.

Anyway, if all fails my senator friend said that Patime could try immigrating to Canada. She said it is actually easier to get permanent residency in Canada than in the United States. After five years of residency and becoming a Canadian citizen, one can go to work in the United States under TN provisions. What are the TN Provisions? They are NAFTA authorizations that allow qualified Canadians and Mexican citizens to stay and work in the United States. But you would have to figure out a way to get Patime across the Canadian border and that may be very challenging. Crossing the border into Canada is tightly controlled by the Canadian government. But Walt, if anyone can figure out a way to get across the border into Canada it would be you.

Walt, when are you leaving for the airport, where are you going and when will you be coming back home? I am leaving for the airport soon and hopefully I will fly back tomorrow night. Walt, that is two out of three. Where are you going? I have a meeting in Newark, New Jersey. Is the meeting with the FBI? No, but it is FBI related. I had a successful meeting in my apartment last night with a nice guy from New Jersey. So please don't worry. I hope you are being candid with me and that you know what you are doing. I am Aunt Harriet. I am doing it my way and I know it is the right thing to do. I am not sure what that means that you will do it your way but I will be anxiously awaiting your telephone call tomorrow night. So please telephone me and Patime before your return flight to Los Angeles. I will Aunt Harriet and tell Patime I will telephone her tomorrow night for sure.

###

Angus when will we meet with Lorenzo? Walt, everyone waits for Lorenzo so hold your horses he will be here soon. He likes straight answers and no "beating around the bush". So, when he asks you a question give him a direct answer. Angus I am not one who avoids answering questions unless I have to lie. But I have no intention of lying to Lorenzo.

So you are Walter Richards, the guy who beat up and shot one of my men. Yes, that is true and I would do it again if I had to. Walt, you need to be more respectful to Lorenzo, you are making a big mistake talking to him like that. Angus shut up. I want to hear what this guy has to say. What do you mean you would do it again? I was protecting my family like you would protect yours and if needed I would do it again. Hmm, I understand. Angus tells me you have some information for me that will let's say help my business. Yes, I do Mr. Rizzo and I think you need to act swiftly or it could be very problematic for you.

Before we get into the information that you may have for me I have a couple of questions. Are you responsible for drugging Angus and having him detained in Mexico for four days? Yes, but there is no way he would have known that I drugged him.

However, he figured it was me who drugged him. Then he found my apartment. He detained me and interrogated me in my apartment and that is why I am here today meeting with you. During his interrogation, he learned that I had been meeting with the FBI and that I had information that would be valuable for you. Are you covering for Angus's mistakes? No of course not. It sounds to me like you might be covering for him. I'm not covering for Angus. Are you sure and you better be straight with me. No, he was quite persuasive with his gun aimed at me. You know I could make things difficult for you if you are lying. No you can't. Walt, you need to be more respectful to Lorenzo and be careful what you are saying. Shut up Angus, I want to hear more of what he has to say before I decide what I want to do with him. I don't mean to be disrespectful Mr. Rizzo but I am being as straight with you as I understand you want me to be. When I said you can't make things difficult for me I meant that you need me as much as I need you. Also, you are being watched by the Feds and they might know that I am here with you. You know Richards you got balls like basketballs but you have my attention.

Okay Richards tell me now why do you want to meet with me? Mr. Rizzo I learned when I was a teenager that when things look bad it is time to look for opportunities. I believe that obstacles make opportunities and they predict one's future. Ricardo is a big obstacle for me and I am not about to let him predict my future. So, when Ricardo unfortunately entered my life and I knew he was up to no good I had to do something to get him out of my life. Why do you need to get Ricardo out of your life? Ricardo came to my parents' home and threatened me and my family. I told him to leave and he pulled a gun on me. I slugged him in the face a few times and then shot his two associates who had guns aimed at me. I don't like it when someone pulls a gun on me. I was incarcerated for nine days and then released with no charges filed against me. However, I have to testify again against Ricardo in his upcoming hearing on June 25th. It appears you had Angus attend Ricardo's and his two associates' preliminary hearings. Then you had Angus follow me to see how I was involved with Ricardo and what I was up to. I now think that Ricardo's two associates Greco and Brown have orders to kill me so that I won't testify against the three of them at their hearings on June 25th. However, I think I have the two of them detained for the time being. But I am certain unless you get involved I will have to deal with them another way when I return to Santa Monica.

Why do you say that you think you have them detained? You either have them detained or not. Mr. Rizzo I know these guys are your soldiers but believe me they are real losers. They are not my soldiers and I don't know anything about them. Ricardo must have hired them, I know I sure didn't. But, go ahead I want to hear more about how you detained them. While parking my car at the airport for my flight to meet with you a minivan pulled up directly behind my parked car. The side sliding door opened and Brown who was bent over had a gun aimed at me. He was too tall to be standing up in the minivan. I said to him you know what happened the last time you aimed a gun at me. He said yes, but this time I am the only one with a gun. Then he ordered me to get into the minivan. I walked up to the sliding door where he was bent over and I threw my tablet computer at him. As he dodged my computer bag I pulled both of his legs outward and he fell down on his back yelling for Greco to help him. I then pulled his legs further out of the van and slugged him in the face one time, well maybe two or three times. I picked up his gun and waited for Greco to get out of the front seat of the van and come help Brown. As Greco came around the back corner of the van I hit him square on the center of his forehead with the butt handle end of Browns gun. He fell down to the ground and I took his gun as well. Then I ordered them both to get in the minivan and take off all their clothes including their underpants. At first Greco said no and so I punched him in the face like I did to Brown. Then they both stripped down completely naked. I emptied the bullets from their guns inside the van, picked up my computer bag, took their clothes and shoes and slid the sliding door of the minivan closed. Then I repeatedly yelled perverts, perverts, perverts. People started surrounding the minivan from the parking lot to see what was happening. I heard the parking lot security police sirens in the background. When I saw that security was getting near I dropped the guns, clothes and shoes in a trash barrel and then got on a shuttle bus to the airport. By the way, my computer still works.

So, when I say I think I have them detained it is because I don't know if Brown and Greco are in jail or are being in custody on a seventy-two hour involuntary mental health hold in a mental ward. Who knows what kind of charges have been filed against them for being naked in the Los Angeles International Airport parking lot in a minivan without any clothes and bullets on the floor of the minivan. But what I do know is at some point they will be after me when I return.

This must have been quite a sight Richards when they got arrested. I am guessing it was Mr. Rizzo but I didn't get to see it because I had a flight to catch to meet with you.

I am impressed with your courage and creativity Richards. So tell me what information you have that you think will be of value to me. I will Mr. Rizzo but I need your assurance that if the information I provide you serves you well that you will get Ricardo, Brown and Greco to leave me and my family alone. Yes, I can agree to that but only if the information is of value to me. If not then there are no assurances. I approved of this meeting with you because Angus told me that the information you have may implicate me in prostitution and sex trafficking and we are not in that kind of business anymore. So, shoot, and tell me what you know. First, I know that your organization no longer wants anything to do with prostitution and certainly not sex trafficking. In fact, I know that you personally executed a policy to terminate all prostitution and sex trafficking in 2012 because Frank Rizzo the former boss was convicted and imprisoned for sex trafficking. I also know that your organization has dwindled significantly in size and is nothing like it was in its heyday. One more big conviction would abolish the family. The Feds know this too and they would like nothing better but to convict you on anything that would eradicate your organization. This leads me to tell you what I know and what you need to know. I broke into Ricardo Sanchez's office a couple of months ago. I found some things in his desk drawer that could incriminate you for sex trafficking. I found a list of names of about fifty young women. It listed their ages, height, weight, the country they came from and a rating for their attractiveness.

I am going to interrupt you Richards. Ricardo is responsible for recruiting girls to work in our two strip clubs in Las Vegas. He has done a good job and business is very good. It would only make sense that he would have such a list in his desk. I understand Mr. Rizzo. But what you need to know is that all of these young women are here in the United States illegally. Ricardo is using their illegal status to coerce them into working in your strip clubs and in some cases being prostitutes. Also, some of these young women are actually girls as young as thirteen years old. This clearly falls under the umbrella of sex trafficking and the Feds currently have Ricardo under surveillance. How do you know they have Ricardo under surveillance? Because they interviewed me while I was in jail and they told me about their surveillance. After I got out of jail I broke into Ricardo's office and stole the list and then I gave it to them. In other words, you might say I have been working with the FBI. I gave the list to them in exchange for a job interview with the FBI. After several days of interviewing me they declined to hire me. I don't think they were ever interested in hiring me but rather they wanted to know what information I could provide about Ricardo and the Rizzo family. I didn't know anything about the Rizzo Family but I did know a lot about Ricardo because I also have been doing a surveillance of him. I learned that he was clearly involved in prostitution.

So, why should I trust you Richards if you are working with the FBI? Because I am not really working with them I only provided them with the list of names. But I have a lot more information that they don't know about and you should. While going through Ricardo's desk I found a file that had communications specifically with you. These letters and notes had photos of some of the young women that were working at your strip clubs. I think he was sending them to you to impress you with how effective he was at recruiting attractive women. But what he didn't tell you in those communications was that the vast majority of them were illegally here in the United States working under the threat of being turned into immigration unless they worked at your strip clubs. Further, he never told you about his side business of illegal prostitution. All of this activity is considered sex trafficking and you could go to prison for a long time.

Is that all or do you have more information? Mr. Rizzo I know and the Feds know that you have a rule number four that specifically states that skimming or doing business on the side is a very serious offence and punishment for doing so is severe. How do you know that Richards? Because I copied a FBI file that dealt with Rizzo Family Sex Trafficking and it contained a historical overview of the Rizzo Family all the way back to Prohibition. It included some letters from one of your accountants Clarence Wilson back in 1960 that had Sammy Rizzo and his underboss Giacamo Vitelli assassinated. I know all about that hit and it severely damaged the business for many years.

Where is that file? I would like to see it. Mr. Rizzo, there is nothing in that file that you don't already know except there is a statement that specifically states that I might try to assassinate you. Are you trying to assassinate me? Of course not Mr. Rizzo. They, like you, are questioning how I got involved with Ricardo Sanchez. Their notation in the FBI file is nothing more than speculation because they don't have any more information about me than you do. Again there is nothing in the file that you don't already know. I will give it to you but I want something in return. What I want from you in return will also serve you well and get you out from under this mess that Ricardo has created for you. I know you don't want to be involved in prostitution and sex trafficking. I am certain that you were not aware of Ricardo's activities in Las Vegas. But it is my expectation that the Feds want to move quickly and secure enough information to indict you within six months and no more than a year. However, I am certain that you can move quicker than the Feds and resolve this problem for yourself within a week or so. Of course you will lose some business in the interim because some of your strippers will have to leave town. But it will pay off in the long run and you will be much better off.

What are you proposing Richards? First, I am giving you the same list of names of the young women that I got from Ricardo's office that I gave to the FBI. All of them are illegally here in the United States and may still be working for you or Ricardo. Some of them may have left Las Vegas but I suspect that most of them are still in Vegas. I suggest you locate those that are still living in Las Vegas. This should not be too difficult because Ricardo knows where they are all living. Then give them each at least $1,000 and tell them to leave Las Vegas immediately and find another place to work and live. Make sure they know you are not threatening them but rather that you are helping them. Explain to them that Immigration is actively hunting for illegal immigrants in Las Vegas. By the way I think this will be true once the FBI turns the list over to Immigration. Immigration will do what they can to round up the young women. I suspect this will happen around the time they try to indict you. However, for the time being the FBI wants to use them as evidence and they have no intention of turning the list over to Immigration. If you do as I am suggesting then you will save the young women from being rounded up and placed in a United States detention camp. Also at the same time you will certainly reduce your accountability and exposure for sex trafficking charges because the evidence will no longer be in Las Vegas. Without the testimony of these young women, the FBI will have no evidence and nothing to charge you with.

I assume you can easily locate the women, pay them, and have them out of town within thirty days. I will then mail you the file that I took from Ricardo's desk that has all the communications with you and the photos of the young women who were working at your strip clubs and possibly involved in prostitution. If this file got in the hands of the Feds it would be very incriminating for you. However, I have no intention of giving this file to them. I know you didn't want to be involved in prostitution and sex trafficking and you didn't know that Ricardo violated your rule number four. I am assuming you only thought he was doing a good job for you in Las Vegas at recruiting strippers and that business was very good.

If you do this I will give you three things. You will immediately get the list of the illegal young women working for you with the exception of one name. It is someone I know and I used a black marker to cover up her name. She has moved far away and you need not find her and give her any money. She is not on your list or the FBI list. You will also get now the FBI Rizzo Family Sex Trafficking file that I copied in their office.

But most importantly, in thirty days I will give you the incriminating file that contains communications between you and Ricardo. It will include letters, notes and photos of the illegal young women working in your strip clubs under duress.

What do you want in return Richards? I want three things. One, I want Ricardo, Greco and Brown out of my life. Two, I don't want to testify on June 25th and three, I would like to catch my flight tonight to Los Angeles. Maybe you could have Angus drive me to the airport.

You got a deal kid, you did well. If everything works out as you have proposed and you need anything we owe you one. Are you still looking for work? With your courage and talents we might be able to use you. Thank you for the offer but I am very happy working at Amazon and I plan on staying there for some time.

I have a question for you Mr. Rizzo. How are you going to preclude me from having to testify and also get Ricardo, Greco and Brown out of my life? Forget about it Richards. I will do it my way. Hmm, I have used that phrase myself Mr. Lorenzo. I bet you have, now get out of here, I have things to do.

###

Angus, your boss does not seem to be as tough as some make him out to be. What do you mean? Well you know when you look at a marshmallow it looks like it could be hard on its sides. But then when you touch it you learn that it is soft. Walt, he may be a little soft but believe me you don't want to cross him.

I don't know if we will meet again Angus but it has been an interesting experience knowing you. Yes, it has Walt and it would be hard to replicate the experience without someone getting seriously hurt and I think it is a tribute to both of us. Angus you are a lot wiser than you look. There you go again kid with your smart-ass wisecracks.

Thanks for the ride Angus and perhaps we will meet again. I doubt it Walt and good luck to you. I have a sense that you will need it.

CHAPTER 14

THE PARENTS

Is this Angus? Yes, who is it? Can you hear me okay? Yes, and I am sorry for the loud background noise but I am working at a casino. Who is this? It is your good friend Walt from Santa Monica. My good friend, I don't think so. Angus we have a lot of history together. If you call drugging me and detaining me at the Mexican border for four days, burning me with pizza and taking my gun you have a strange definition of a good friend and history. I know Angus but I told you no one ever pulls a gun on me and gets away with it. Yes, I learned that Walt. How are you Walt? I am doing very well. So, I am guessing you gave up your job at Amazon as an Amazon driver and now you are working at a casino in Vegas. No, Angus I am still driving for Amazon but only part-time. Are you working at a casino the other part of the time as a dealer? No, I am not. I started a security surveillance business that specializes in the facial recognition of known felons. It has nothing to do with the gambling business but it alerts a casino of someone entering the casino that has a criminal history. I guess Walt it would catch me. I suppose it would Angus.

What can I do for you Walt? First, I want to thank you and Lorenzo again for taking care of my Ricardo Sanchez problem back in 2018. I don't know what you all did and I don't care. But I am very appreciative that I didn't have to testify at the court hearing and I am over with having to deal with Ricardo. Good and you know Walt, you saved Lorenzo's ass. He is very appreciative that your plan worked. The Feds never filed any charges and business is back to normal in Vegas. In fact, business is very good. This is the reason I am calling you Angus. Lorenzo told me at our meeting back then in Newark that if my plan getting the Feds off his back worked he owed me one. I don't think he owes me anything. But I am hoping you can help me with a problem. What's the problem? I might need some passports or visas. Do you think you can help? How many people? There is a man and a woman and they are both about forty-five years old. Walt it depends on the country. What country is it? Well there are three possible countries in Asia. They are China, Kyrgyzstan and Tajikistan. What kind of stan? I know about China but never heard of the stans. Kyrgyzstan and Tajikistan are countries near the west of China's border. I know I can pretty easily get passports for parts of Western Europe like Luxembourg, Portugal and Italy but Asia I don't know. Do you have photos of the man and the woman? No. Then Walt I don't think we can help you at all without photos. That's okay Angus I thought I would give it a long shot and ask you to see if you could help.

Thanks for your time Angus and I hope life is treating you well. I now live in Vegas full time so if you are ever here come meet my wife and the twins. You got married? Yes, I did and the four of us are very happy here. You should come for dinner and maybe have some pizza. I am just joking Angus. I really would like you to meet my wife and kids. Where did you meet your wife? I kind of met her at Amazon. What do you mean by you kind of met her at Amazon? You either did or didn't meet her at Amazon. It's a long story about a package that I will tell you about sometime when I see you in person.

###

Excuse me sir, are you an American? No. Oh, I am guessing from your accent you are English. No, I am Australian. Sorry, I can never tell the difference. It is a common mistake made by Americans. My name is Walt Richards and I am trying to find someone here in Bishkek and you looked like you might know your way around. Don't you really mean that I don't look anything like the locals? Yes, that too but I sensed you were not a tourist and that you were familiar with Bishkek. Well, you are right about that, I am here on long term business. My name is Sean Williamson and I am from Sydney. How long have you been here in Kyrgyzstan? I have been living here in Bishkek for over two months and I return to Sidney in three weeks. What kind of business do you do here in Bishkek? Copper. The company I work for in Sydney makes copper wire of all sizes and copper is one of the things that favorably drives Kyrgyzstan's economy. Copper is a hot commodity worldwide because it is widely used in technology. Actually, I am not alone as an Australian here in Kyrgyzstan. There is an Australian expat community living here long term. My company has a factory in Bishkek and I come here on business every year for a few months.

Why are you here Walt? I will tell you, but how about I buy you lunch or a beer and we can talk about it then? Sure, that sounds good. I know a great place nearby that makes lagham. What is lagham? Lagham is a prepared meat usually made with lamb or beef in a sauce. It has vegetables, pulled long noodles, peppers, eggplant, radish, potatoes, onion, garlic and lots of spices. It is really quite good and it is my favorite dish here in Bishkek. It will fill you up for the day.

Did you like the lagham Walt? I did but I am not a fan of bell peppers. Next time you order it ask for it without the bell pepper. I am sure that they can do that for you. So, tell me Walt why are you here in Bishkek? I am looking for my wife's parents. Give me their address and I can take you there. I don't have their address. They are Uyghur and I have information that they may have very recently fled from Xinjiang, China looking for their daughter. They think their daughter lives here in Bishkek but she lives in the States with me. It is a long story but they have been separated now for several years and I am here to find them. Walt, it seems like everyone is trying to find something or someone in Bishkek. The government is looking for alleged terrorists, the police are looking for criminals, family members are looking for lost relatives and people are looking for food and work.

How long have they lived here Walt? I think if they are in fact living here then they would only have been here for a few weeks. What is their surname? Do you mean their last name? Yes. In the States we don't normally ask people their surname we ask for their last name. There are lots of things you do in the States that are strange to me. Anyway what is their last name? Their last name is Abdulla. Abdulla is a pretty common name Walt, especially in the city of Bishkek. It is a common Muslim name. It can be spelled Abdulla and Abdullah with an H on the end of the name. How is your Abdulla spelled? Without the H. That might help a bit. What are their first names? My wife's mother's name is Arzu Abdulla and her father is Erkin Abdulla. What makes you think they are here in Bishkek? I am not one hundred percent sure but they are Uyghur and there is a rather large Uyghur community in Bishkek. Walt, you need to know that there are many Uyghurs living here who are legal and some that are illegal. Both legal and illegal Uyghurs sometimes prefer keeping to themselves or remaining anonymous. Many fear repercussions. What do you mean by repercussions? There is fear here with Uyghurs that they will be persecuted because of their culture and heritage. They only make up one percent of Kyrgyzstan's population and they are Muslim like ninety percent of the country. However, they have been falsely targeted as terrorists and most of the Uyghur community lives here in Bishkek.

You probably know that authorities in Xinjiang, China are sentencing Muslim Kyrgyzstan people to reeducation centers for "religious violations" along with Uyghurs living in the region. The persecution of Uyghurs by the Chinese government is by far the worst but it is also happening to other Muslim minorities in China. You might say that China is an equal opportunity oppressor. Yes, I know all about this and my wife escaped from a reeducation camp a few years ago. It was really a labor detention camp with horrible conditions. My wife has emotional scars from the horrific experience that she endured during her three months imprisonment in the detention camp.

I am sorry to hear that Walt. The situation here is not as bad as Xinjiang but it is not good. There are serious problems here for Uyghurs. There are stories of long prison sentences for committing minor crimes. However, comparatively Kyrgyzstan is seen as a safe haven for many Uyghurs. But it is not totally safe. Chinese political and economic influence in Kyrgyzstan has risen substantially. As bilateral ties have strengthened, authorities have upped their surveillance and repression of Uyghurs. In recent years, authorities have frequently prohibited Uyghur travel because they have been targeted as terrorists.

I read Walt, that tensions affecting Uyghurs here in Bishkek may be connected more to local interethnic issues than top-down repression by the government. But I don't know if this is true or not. Sometime ago there were sporadic reports of Uyghurs being targeted by mobs. A Uyghur favorite restaurant here in Bishkek was torched. In that year a Uyghur dominated bazaar in Bishkek was burnt to the ground during several hours of ethnic violence. Also some time ago the World Uyghur Congress in Bishkek extradited fifty Uyghurs to China on supposedly trumped-up terrorism charges.

So you see Walt, the conditions here in Kyrgyzstan are not great but they are better than in China. We don't have detention camps but we do have persecutions of the Uyghur people. I don't know how you are going to find your wife's parents but a good place might be to check the three mosques in Bishkek.

Where are you staying while here in Bishkek. I don't have a place yet but I read that hotel prices are very reasonable. Yes, they are Walt. Where are you staying? I have a long-term room at the Hyatt hotel because my company is paying for it. But there are a lot of cheaper places that you will find nice and clean. Here is my cell phone number if you need to talk. Thanks for all the information.

###

I am sorry to bother you and I am hoping you can help me. I understand that you are the Imam for this mosque. My name is Walter Richards and I am trying to locate Arzu and Erkin Abdulla. Do you know them? No, I don't think so. They recently came here from Xinjiang. No, I am sorry I don't know them. Why are you looking for them? They are my wife's parents and I am from the States looking for them. I am sorry I don't know them but we have three mosques here in Bishkek maybe someone would know them at another mosque. I understand and I will go to the other mosques but maybe you can still help. My wife's parents who are Uyghurs we think recently escaped from Xinjiang and came here within the past few weeks. Mr. Richards, there are a lot of people who come here from Xinjiang and some do their best to keep anonymous and out of the way. There have been some government officials recently who have stated that there are Uyghur terrorists in Bishkek. We have had incidents of Uyghurs here being targeted in bazaars and shopping areas as a danger to society. I know this but I believe they came here to look for my wife who they thought was here in Bishkek because she had been missing for some time. I can assure you they are not terrorists. They are simply looking for their lost daughter. Mr. Richards I didn't mean to imply that your wife's parents are terrorists but rather I want you to know that conditions here for Uyghurs can be problematic. Thank you but any piece of information you may provide may be a big help in my locating her parents.

Mr. Richards do you have a photo of your wife's parents? No, unfortunately I don't. I am sorry then Mr. Richards I don't think I can be of any help and I suggest you try another mosque where they might know them. The Uyghur community is quite tight and maybe someone at another mosque can be of help. But before you go you need to know that I have members of this mosque who have lived here in Bishkek for some time. One for example is Aigul, my sister-in-law. She was able to leave her native region of Xinjiang seven years ago to study at a university in her ancestral homeland here in Kyrgyzstan. When she arrived she changed her name because she had personal security concerns. To this date she still lives in fear of persecution by Chinese officials. So, you see your wife's parents may have also changed their names and without more information or photos it may be very difficult or even impossible to find them. I appreciate the information you have provided and I will remember what you said about security concerns. Thank you very much for your time.

###

Hello Sean, it is me Walt. Would you like to meet for lunch again? Yes, is everything okay? Yes, but I may have a problem that I would like to discuss with you over lunch and this time I will buy. How about the same place that we got the lagham last time? That sounds good. See you at noon.

The reason I wanted to meet with you is that I may have a problem and I am not sure what to do about it in this foreign country. What is the problem Walt? I met with an Imam several days ago at the central city mosque. Although he tried to help me find my wife's parents he couldn't. He suggested that I go to the mosque on the western side of Bishkek which I did.

While I was walking to the mosque a car slowly pulled up directly in front of me and a guy got out from the front passenger seat of a car. He then ran up to a lady who was walking on the sidewalk adjacent to the car and he snatched her purse. He tugged her purse so hard that she fell to the ground. He then started to get back into the car with her purse as the driver waited. I was close enough that I was able to pull him by the collar of his shirt and he fell to the street. He pulled a gun on me and I hit him in the face one time. Well, maybe two or three times. I don't like it when someone pulls a gun on me. Anyway, I took his gun and the purse and he dragged himself back into the car and then they sped off.

I returned the purse to the lady who wasn't badly hurt but she was very appreciative. Were the police involved? No. Good it is probably better that they aren't involved. You could be interviewed and detained and you don't need that if you are looking for your wife's parents who are most likely illegally here in Kyrgyzstan. That is what I thought. So, I thought I would call you before going to the police and get your opinion since you are familiar with how things work here. Purse snatchings and pickpockets are common here Walt and it is best not to get involved. Guns are highly regulated here but there are still some guns on the streets. I don't think going to the police is advisable. Where is the gun now Walt? I have it with me in my coat pocket. You need to get rid of the gun. Give it to me and I will take care of it for you after lunch.

There is more. Sean. It appears the lady has money and position and she must have been a target rather than a random purse snatching. I told her about my looking for my wife's parents and she wants to help me. I am meeting with her and some of her friends the day after tomorrow for dinner at her home. Walt do you think this is wise? I was a little skeptical about it at first but after I learned that her husband Stephen Kastenblatt develops property in the city and she is involved in some human rights issues I then felt it was safe to meet and have dinner. Do you want me to go with you? No, I can handle this on my own. But, I do appreciate your getting rid of the gun for me.

###

Everyone I want to introduce you to Mr. Walter Richards from the United States. He courageously helped me out a couple of days ago and I told him that I would try to help him find his wife's parents. They are from Xinjiang. Walter thinks that they illegally left Xinjiang to look for their daughter in Kyrgyzstan. Actually, she lives in the United States with Walter. She escaped from a Uyghur detention camp a few years ago and the family has completely lost touch with her. They somehow got information that their daughter was here in Bishkek so they fled Xinjiang and came here looking for her. They are about forty-five years old and their names are Arzu and Erkin Abdulla. So, I am asking you when you go home could you please ask around with your family and friends if they know anyone by the name of Arzu or Erkin Abdulla who recently came to Bishkek.

Saliha, it just so happens I may have some information that might be helpful. I don't know the surname but I do know that a woman by the name of Arzu is being cared for in a hospital near the central mosque here in Bishkek. A farmer who I do business with told me that several days ago he was driving on the G7 at night and found a couple on the side of the road who had been in a motorcycle accident. It appears the headlight on their motorcycle failed and they hit a pothole in the road and lost control of their motorcycle. He told me that the man must have died instantly on the spot from a broken neck. But the woman was alive and being treated at a hospital for severe lacerations to the head and neck. I don't know her condition but I think she is still alive.

Thank you Omar this is very helpful and I will take Walter to the hospital in the morning. If it is okay with you Saliha can you take me now? Yes, of course Walter we will go right away.

CHAPTER 15

KYRGYZSTAN

Marian and Pete thank you for watching the kids. Walt will be home by dinner time and then he can take over. I will only be gone for a day and one half. Don't worry about anything while you are gone. We look forward to and enjoy taking care of the grandkids. It will be more fun than work. So please don't worry. Will someone be accompanying you on your flight to Washington D.C.? Yes, a woman I really like from Amnesty International. She has been with me at a couple of my prior Senate hearings and I find her very helpful.

###

Good morning Senator and I hope you are well today. I am well Mrs. Richards and I trust that life is continuing to treat you better each day now that you have your Green Card. Yes, Senator it is and I hope I can be of value today with my testimony. You have been sworn in and we have the hearing room reserved for the entire day for the subcommittee. Although, I don't think you need an interpreter we have one available as we have had at all your prior hearings.

I think Mrs. Richards that this is your third appearance before our subcommittee on human trafficking. I understand that you have also testified at a bipartisan committee that is spearheading a bill to ensure that goods made in Uyghur forced labor camps in Xinjiang, China are precluded from entering the United States. I assume you know this but it is the conclusion of both our committees that the

Chinese Communist Party is committing crimes against humanity and genocide against Uyghurs and other Muslim minorities in Xinjiang. Amnesty International has provided our Committee with a report that includes a proposed action plan. The 160-page report is titled, "Like We Were Enemies in a War": China's Mass Internment, Torture, and Persecution of Muslims in Xinjiang". Amnesty International's Crisis Response team released dozens of new testimonies like yours from former detainees. These testimonies detail the extreme measures taken by Chinese authorities since 2017 to essentially root out the religious traditions, cultural practices, and local languages of the region's Muslim ethnic groups. This effort by the Chinese government has been carried out under the guise of fighting "terrorism" but we know better.

Yes senator, I do know the positions and conclusions of both committees and I have read the report. However, for clarification this is my fourth appearance before your subcommittee and not my third. My first appearance was very brief back in August 2018. A Senate Bill was being approved authorizing a Green Card for me because of my illegal status in the United States. I testified briefly at that hearing to thank the Senate for approving the bill and giving me legal authorization to stay in the United States. I am pleased to announce that because my husband is a United States citizen and we were married on October 31, 2018, I can apply for citizenship under the "three-year rule" next Halloween on October 31, 2021. Applicants who are married to a United States citizen can file for citizenship after three years rather than unmarried applicants who have to wait five years. Will that be a trick or treat for you Mrs. Richards? I am just joking Mrs. Richards, I know it will definitely be a treat. Yes, it will be a treat Senator and the date has a lot of meaning to my husband and me. I bet it does Mrs. Richards and we are all very happy for you.

Mrs. Richards I am going to now summarize what you testified to at your other three hearings for the record and to refresh the committee. You testified to the atrocities that were committed in the labor camp where you and your sister were detained. Again, I am sorry for the loss of your sister and I won't have you revisit the abuses you endured or pursue any questions about the "black room". You also described at one of the hearings how you escaped in the belly of an airplane headed for Los Angeles. You testified that it was your belief that if you hadn't escaped then you would have been placed in the sex trafficking business. At your last hearing, you described the actual physical conditions of the detention camp you lived in for three months and the work that was performed by the detainees to make textile goods.

We have all the details we need for this committee from you on human trafficking. However, I have an important question to ask you about the detention camps. Can you tell us how many detention camps you think there are in Xinjiang, China? I am sorry Senator I cannot give you a specific number. But I read that In September 2020, the Australian Strategic Policy Institute launched its Xinjiang Data Project which reported that the construction of camps continued despite claims that their function was winding down. They identified three hundred and eighty camps and detention centers. It is believed that the Chinese government had arbitrarily detained more than a million Muslims in reeducation camps since 2017. This is when my sister and I were first detained. Most of the people who have been detained are Uyghurs which as you know is a predominantly Trick-speaking ethnic minority primarily living in China's northwestern region of Xinjiang. In these camp Uyghurs are under intense surveillance, forced labor, involuntary sterilizations and other human rights abuses. The Chinese government calls these camps vocational education training centers but they are nothing more than internment camps and many have forced labor as part of their “reeducation” program.

At your last two hearings Mrs. Richards you testified on the living conditions, the beatings and what you believed to be an organized sex trade operation in the camp where you were detained in Xinjiang. You stated that you didn’t know if these conditions were in other detention camps. But you testified that you were certain that there were human rights abuses in all the camps because Uyghurs were all being detained against their will.

For today’s hearing we would like you to address the ways and means Uyghurs’ escape from Xinjiang. Specifically, we would like to know where do they hide or go as refugees.

This is a complicated answer Senator because there isn’t really anyplace reasonable for them to escape. If you look at a map of China and the nearest countries which are to the west you will find Kyrgyzstan and Tajikistan are the closest. Kyrgyzstan is about seven hundred miles by car but it is almost impossible to leave because the Chinese government restricts the movement of Uyghurs. Going by bus is about thirty-six hours but getting past checkpoints is virtually impossible. Although Kyrgyzstan is probably the most welcoming of the two countries it is not ideal. Both Kyrgyzstan and Tajikistan are under economic and social pressure by the Chinese government to restrict Uyghurs from entering their countries. Tajikistan is about four hundred miles further than Kyrgyzstan and more difficult to get to than Kyrgyzstan.

During your last testimony Mrs. Richards you indicated that you and your husband were going to try something new to contact or find your parents in Xinjiang. You said that he was working on a plan. If I recall correctly you have not seen or heard from your parents since July 15, 2017 when you and your sister were abducted in front of your family home in Xinjiang and taken to the detention camp. Can you please share with us what you are doing to find your parents? Yes Senator, I would be happy to share it with you but this is very emotional for me and I hope I can contain my emotions during my testimony. Mrs. Richards please take all the time you need.

I miss my parents very much and I have not had any way of communicating with them for the past few years. I have tried everything. I have sent letters to them and people we knew in Xinjiang and had no response. I suspect that the government has been confiscating my letters but I can't confirm this. I have tried to telephone them but I think that their original cell phone was taken from them when I escaped in October of 2017. I assumed they may have gotten a new cell phone and cell phone number. But I don't really know and I can't find any cell phone number for them with their names. We considered hiring someone to search for them in Xinjiang. However, we realized we had two problems with this plan. One, if we did hire someone we wouldn't really know if we could trust the person. Two, it might make my parents situation worse than it already might be.

I did not know if my parents were dead or alive. Further, they don't know what happened to me. It bothers me deeply so my husband decided that he would go to Xinjiang and see if he could find them on his own. He is a very courageous person and he has a way with getting things done. He told me jokingly "I will do it my way" but he was not joking. What does that mean Mrs. Richards? Well, it means that he will be creative and bring the situation to a conclusion no matter what it takes. When he has his mind set on something he gets things done. He tells me that to try is to presume failure and that obstacles should be looked at as opportunities for change. He says that too many people see obstacles as a roadblock when in fact, it can be an opportunity for change rather than letting the obstacle predict ones future.

So a few weeks ago my husband flew to Xinjiang to find my parents. His first stop was of course our family home in Xinjiang. I described our home in detail to my husband. I even drew pictures so that he could find our home. Our home was not large or fancy. It was a typically constructed mud-brick and timber home with a small outdoor courtyard area with vegetation growing on the trellises. He had no difficulty finding our home and learned that my parents were no longer living there. The new residents said that my parents only weeks earlier left for Kyrgyzstan to find me. According to the new resident, someone supposedly told my parents I was alive and living in Kyrgyzstan. Who told them this I don't know. Maybe someone wanted our family home and simply wanted them to leave Xinjiang so that it would be vacated. Maybe, someone really thought that I was living in Kyrgyzstan. Or, maybe there is someone who looks like me and they were mistaken about me living in Kyrgyzstan. I will never know but what I do know is that my parents believed that I was alive and living in Kyrgyzstan and they went to find me. Prior to their learning that I might be in Kyrgyzstan, my parents had no idea if I was still alive or where I might be living. The last piece of information they had about me was in October 2017 when they gave money to a Chinese couple who were going to take me out of the detention camp and supposedly to safety in Turkey. But as you know they didn't take me to Turkey but rather they wanted to use or sell me in the sex trade business. I escaped from them and illegally came to the United States in the belly of an airplane.

My husband said that the new residents of our home could not provide any other information. He asked them if they had heard any rumors about me being sold in the sex trade business. They said repeatedly the only thing they heard was that I escaped somehow to Kyrgyzstan from the detention camp and may be in Bishkek.

My husband believed them and decided to go to Kyrgyzstan to find my parents. He felt it might be safer for him to join a tourist group and go to Kyrgyzstan as a cover for looking for my parents. He didn't know what the conditions would be like so he joined a short tour that was studying the history of the Silk Road.

Can you remind us Mrs. Richards what is the Silk Road? Briefly, the Silk Road was a network of paths created in 130 B.C.E connecting civilizations in the East and West that was well traveled for 1,500 years. Merchants on the Silk Road transported goods and traded at bazaars along the way. According to my husband it is of significant historical importance. Anyway, when he got to Kyrgyzstan he immediately went to the main Uyghur community in Bishkek.

My husband spent a total of ten days in Bishkek. He finally met a woman who introduced him to a man who knew something about my parents. The man knew of a farmer who was driving on one of the main roads several hours away from Bishkek. The farmer said that he was driving his flatbed truck on the main road at night when he saw a man lying on the ground with a woman bent over him crying. He said that the two of them were trying to get to Bishkek on a motorcycle to find me. It appears his motorcycle headlight burnt out, they hit a pothole in the dark and the motorcycle went out of control. The farmer said that the man must have broken his neck and died instantly on the spot.

Mrs. Richards are you sure this man was your father? Yes, I am and my husband has since found my mother. I am so very sorry Mrs. Richards about your loss of your father and I think this would be a good time to recess. We are in recess for thirty minutes and all please return by noon.

Are you able to continue Mrs. Richards? Yes, I am. Again I am sorry for your loss and please continue if you can. The farmer put my father in the back of his flatbed truck with the mangled motorcycle. He helped my mother into the cab of the truck. She had severe lacerations on her head and neck and she had lost a lot of blood. My mother begged the farmer not to take her to the hospital but rather to take her to a Uyghur doctor that could be trusted in Bishkek.

They drove for several hours and the man then took my mother to a Uyghur doctor that was very trusted by the community. He did his best to care for her but she had to be hospitalized. She got sepsis from infections and died about a week later.

I am so sorry Mrs. Richards. This must also be terrible for you to talk about learning that your mother and father both died looking for you. Yes, it is terribly painful but my husband found my mother before she died. He sat by her side at the hospital for three days until she slipped into a coma and died. Before she died he was able to tell her about how he found me in the back of his Amazon van and he showed her pictures of me and her grandchildren the twins. At least she knew that I was alive, safe and that she finally found me. She gave my husband the locket that I am wearing on my neck today which has a photograph of my sister Patime and me together when we were very young. It is the only photo or thing that I have of my family and I will cherish it forever.

Thank you Patime, I mean Amatullah Richards, we do appreciate your testimony. Hopefully, your testimony will serve our two committees well and we can legislate some changes to protect Uyghurs and thwart human rights abuses.

Before you go I have a couple of personal questions if you don't mind me asking. First, how is it reverting to your birth name Amatullah and not using Abdulla and Patime as your first name? You know Senator when I first met my husband he couldn't pronounce my first name Amatullah. But he had no problem calling me by my last name Abdulla. My English was very poor back then and it was difficult for me to clarify my name with him so I went along with it and had him call me Abdulla rather than Amatullah. Actually, Abdulla is a very common boy's first name and a surname as well. It means servant of Allah. When I went into hiding at my Aunt Harriet's in San Bernardino I had to change my name. I selected the name Patime in honor of my sister who died in the detention camp. I got very used to it and even liked it. But now I am very glad to be using my birth name that my parents gave me-Amatullah.

My other question is how are the twins? They are both almost two years old now and quite a handful. My daughter Patime seems to be quicker at learning to talk than my son Abdulla. But Abdulla like his dad is more driven to get things done than his sister Patime. But they are both healthy and safe which is more important than anything else to me. Is your husband caring for the twins while you are here in Washington D.C.? They are being cared for by his parents in Las Vegas until he gets home from work. What kind of work does he do? He has recently started a security facial recognition business. Until that business gets fully up and running he is an Amazon driver.

EPILOGUE

"We must always take sides. Neutrality helps the oppressor, never the victim. Silence encourages the tormentor, never the tormented. Sometimes we must interfere. When human lives are endangered, when human dignity is in jeopardy, national borders and sensitivities become irrelevant. Wherever men or women are persecuted because of their race, religion, or political views, that place must—at that moment—become the center of the universe."

Elie Wiesel
Nobel Peace Prize Acceptance Speech, December 10, 1986.

Books by James Ellman

The Amazon Driver

The Butcher, The Baker, The Candlestick Maker, The Uber Driver And 36 Other Short Stories

Made in the USA
Las Vegas, NV
06 August 2023

75721272R00121